SEARCHING FOR SCARLETT

It's 1995 and newly promoted Detective Constable Kimberly Frost is thrown in at the deep end with a double child abduction case to solve — then is struck down with a health condition that leaves her struggling to communicate. Even worse is the way that the kidnapper seems to know her every move. The criminal is clearly a whizz with computers but luckily so is her childhood pal Mark, whose unfailing support is complicated by his desire to become more than just a friend. How will Kimberly cope with it all?

Books by Alan C. Williams
in the Linford Romance Library:

CHRISTMAS DOWN UNDER
LOST IN THE OUTBACK

ALAN C. WILLIAMS

SEARCHING FOR SCARLETT

Complete and Unabridged

LINFORD
Leicester

First published in Great Britain in 2019

First Linford Edition
published 2020

A catalogue record for this book is available
from the British Library.

ISBN 978–1–4448–4461–0

Published by
Ulverscroft Limited
Anstey, Leicestershire

Set by Words & Graphics Ltd.
Anstey, Leicestershire
Printed and bound in Great Britain by
T. J. International Ltd., Padstow, Cornwall

This book is printed on acid-free paper

1

It was the eighth of December, 1995; the first day. Four hours ago, Crystal and Scarlett Bowen had been reported missing.

Initial indications suggested an abduction. It was our job to find the young sisters and bring them home safely.

A large number of police, uniforms and plain clothes, were searching the area or asking questions of neighbours and friends. Forensics had already left. It was a major incident, especially in the normally sedate county of Herefordshire.

Most of the Detective Inspectors were involved in other cases, including murders. Our own DI was out co-ordinating the search, which was the reason Detective Sergeant Cameron was asked to help out with the crime scene.

My first week as a Detective Constable had been relatively quiet until today; a number of burglaries, an escaped prisoner re-arrested and some graffiti sprayed on the side of a church.

Mum was really proud of my promotion; Dad less so.

'Kimberly,' he'd said on discovering I'd applied to the Force. 'With that degree of yours and those brains, you could achieve so much more than being a copper.' That attitude hadn't changed, even with me becoming a detective.

I used to be Daddy's little angel. It wasn't as though he had any other children. You'd think he'd make the effort, but . . .

'DC Frost. Are you taking this down?'

'Yes, Sergeant.' It was a good thing I could multi-task.

'Radio the names through to the station. Maybe they can help. Then I want you to come with me to the girls' bedroom. You might spot some clue I'd

2

miss . . . being a woman and all.'

'Yes, Sergeant.' I ignored the patronising comment. My brief was to watch and listen, not to speak unless spoken to. That suited me right now. Being a detective was a whole new ball game compared to uniform.

Even so, I felt I was back in school with Miss Diamond giving me one of her lengthy lectures on being too talkative in lessons. At least I didn't have a funny smile like she did.

I'd learned a great deal about people and their behaviour at school. I'd studied body language from books, then put it into practice as a police officer, making a bit of a name for myself as a thief taker.

One advantage of being a detective was no longer having to make tea and coffee for the mainly male staff at HQ. Life for women was improving, though too slowly for me. More than once I'd been warned about my sardonic attitude.

Having given the names to our

station incident co-ordinator, DS Cameron and I accompanied a distraught Candice Bowen to the girls' bedroom. It was large and lavishly decorated with My Little Pony wallpaper and bedlinen, the sisters' names printed above their beds in gold lettering.

As they were just five and three, I didn't expect to find much in the way of clues; no diaries or photos with secret boyfriends. Nevertheless, there might be signs as to who had taken them. Forensics had been and gone, with evidence about possible identities of the intruders who'd snatched them under cover of the chilly night.

There were two of them. Their muddy footprints were all over the carpets. Men, by the shoe sizes.

Mrs Bowen, still wearing her dressing gown and rollers, just stood in the doorway, sobbing, her tear-stained face and blank expression conveying her anguish. Her two angels were gone.

There was the faintest whiff of chloroform tainting the warm air.

'Notice anything yet, DC Frost?'

'The bedclothes. Arranged neatly as though whoever took them was fastidious. Almost as if they were re-making the beds.'

'The forensics team might have done that.'

My superior was testing me, I suspected.

'No. I saw the photos taken when officers first arrived. There's no reason for the intruders to have done that unless it was habit. Military?'

DS Cameron nodded. 'Worth considering.'

I opened another drawer neatly packed with tiny blouses and underwear. I felt like an intruder myself. Then I spied a reflected gleam from the side of a Teddy Ruxpin toy — my friend's sister had one. The object was caught under a furry paw.

'Sergeant?' I pointed. He carefully retrieved it with gloved fingers. It was a silver ring.

'Does this belong in this house?' he

asked Mrs Bowen. She examined it and shook her head.

'The criminals?' I suggested as he placed it in a plastic evidence bag, after writing on the label.

'Unlikely, DC Frost. They were wearing gloves so there's no reason for one to have dropped it.

'Perhaps one needed to remove his glove to open the chloroform? Opening small bottles is awkward at the best of times.'

Sergeant Cameron studied the item, pensively. 'Man's ring. Some inscription. Latin or something. In any case, well done for finding it. Those Forensic fellas think they're so thorough. Might help us find the girls — but it's not much to go on.'

He glanced over to Candice. She appeared so distant. Her husband was on his way back from Bonn. However right now she was alone, coping with a mother's worst nightmare.

My boss nudged me.

'DC Frost . . . Kimberly. Don't

'spose you could do us all a cuppa?'

Some things never changed. Still, he was right. It might assist her even if it was a distraction.

On the way out, I asked for Candice's preferences and where the kitchen was. Her answers were in a monotone, her eyes fixed on her daughters' empty beds.

Once in the hallway, I realised how vast this home was. Vague footprints indicated the intruders' movement along the long passageway. Imprints had been taken but, even so, I avoided stepping on them.

The sprawling corridors were more suited to some posh hotel. It was single-storey, built recently, with mod-cons like vacuum outlets set into the skirting and bronze-hued intercoms on the walls. Forty-odd acres of fields and woodlands surrounded this secluded paradise. Officers were searching the gravelled tracks nearby for a sign of the vehicle the kidnappers must have used.

Walking briskly to the kitchen, I

decided to prepare a sandwich for Mrs Bowen or at least find some biscuits. She probably hadn't eaten.

'Damn,' I said, opening a door to some sort of study. It was supposed to be the dining room leading through to the kitchen. I tried the next one. It contained a full-sized snooker table with cues in their racks standing to attention.

'It's like a maze,' I exclaimed out loud. The next door seemed more promising.

How had the criminals found their way so unerringly from the utility room to the girls' bedroom? The footprint impressions showed no deviations or stumbling into the wrong room.

Then there was the alarm. Mrs Bowen had been unsure if she'd set it. She'd dosed herself up on some medicines the night before.

Another door led into a massive kitchen. Talk about mod-cons. The signs of a half-prepared breakfast for three littered the marble-topped bench and bar. Clearly, she'd dropped every-thing when she discovered the girls had vanished.

I set about preparing drinks with some food. The kitchen alone was probably half the size of the terraced place I was renting.

Just as I was about to return with a laden tray, I noticed something odd written on the edge of the Advent calendar. I made a mental note before retracing my steps to the children's bedroom.

My boss was gently trying to reassure Candice. It seemed awkward for him. He wasn't one of those touchy-feely people. She needed someone to hug her, to reassure her it would be all right. Sadly DS Steven Cameron wasn't that individual.

Putting the tray down, I took over. Not that I was a mother. I was twenty-five, though I wasn't thinking of marriage or starting a family as yet. As for my boyfriend, Barry, I had no idea if he even wanted kids. We'd been going out for a few months, but never discussed plans for the future.

There were no words I could say to ease Mrs Bowen's pain, but at least I could embrace her and comfort her as wracking sobs made her body shudder under my arms.

I didn't rush her. She was a strong woman, in spite of her present distress. Soon the realisation that she needed to find that strength again, to do whatever she could to find her darlings, allowed her to focus.

As the heaving gasps subsided, I offered her some sweet tea. The sergeant and I helped her to an armchair.

'Thank you,' she said, placing her hand on mine. 'Kimberly, is it? A lovely name.'

I could sense DS Cameron was pleased I'd taken over. He swept back the lock of chocolate-brown hair that had fallen across his forehead. His moustache and goatee were straight out of those halcyon days of the Seventies.

He and his wife had one son and, in the few days I'd worked closely with him, I'd found him to be kind and compassionate as well as a decent copper through and through. Experienced, too.

He'd seen his own share of victims trying to cope, I guessed. It would have been easy to detach in order to cope with the continual immersion in the worst aspects of humanity. To his credit, his feelings for the victims were still there. They showed in his saddened eyes.

'Mrs Bowen . . . ' I began.

'Call me Candice, please.'

'Candice. There was a note out there on the Advent calendar, in the kitchen.'

She took a sip of her drink and bit into a proffered sandwich.

'Who's Jessica?' I inquired. 'She wasn't on the list of relatives and contacts you gave us.'

Her mind took a moment to focus on my query.

'Jessica? Oh — yes. Our former

housekeeper. I had to dismiss her. Stealing.'

DS Cameron came over. He'd realised the implications immediately.

'Why didn't you mention her earlier?' he casually asked Candice.

She shook her head. 'I forgot. She's a teenager — doted on the girls, always joking with them, pulling funny faces. She bought the calendar as a present.'

That explained the inscription.

'She wouldn't be involved in this. I'm absolutely sure of that,' Candice added emphatically.

'Could you tell us what she stole?' Steven prompted.

'Some money. I'd set up a video camera when I noticed the odd missing item from the lounge area. I felt bad about not trusting her, though I was proved right in the end. But theft is one thing, DS Cameron. She loved my girls too much to do anything like this.'

Nevertheless, Steven seemed quietly elated.

'You have a camera set up?'

'Switched it off when Jessica left. It wouldn't have helped. It was over the other side of the house.'

Glancing at my boss, I saw him mouth 'Good work' to me. A disgruntled employee, no matter how much she adored the girls, was certainly a suspect worth pursuing. It would explain the possible alarm deactivation, the break-in via the faulty window and the apparent knowledge of the direct route to the girl's room.

There were footsteps in the hall. We turned to see that the family liaison officer had arrived. I'd worked with her as a uniformed officer. She was professional yet compassionate.

'The phone's all set up, DS Cameron. Just in case anyone rings with information.'

I knew she meant the kidnappers, although there was no point in upsetting Candice any more.

'Would you have the address and full name of this Jessica, please?' DS Cameron asked. 'DC Frost and I might have a word with her — just to eliminate her from our enquiries.'

★　★　★

In a way, it was good to get away from the house. I'd felt so helpless there. At least, going to Jessica's home would be doing something to find Scarlett and Crystal.

True, it was a long shot. Candice had valid reasons for sacking Jessica yet she was adamant that her home-help had been fond of the kids.

It was a ten-minute drive back to the suburbs of Hereford.

'Pound for your thoughts, Kimberly,' said DS Cameron. He'd insisted on driving, which suited me. My own car was much less powerful than most of the unmarked vehicles at the station.

'A pound? What happened to a penny?'

'Inflation,' he explained. 'Bet you weren't born when we had pounds, shillings and pence. Sometimes I do miss the old days. No one would snatch kids back then, even the hardened crims hereabouts. I have to say that was a good spot you made regarding this Jessica girl. Still . . . talking to her? It'll probably be nothing.'

I realised our destination wasn't far away now. Hereford wasn't that large and, although I'd only lived here a few years, I could find my way around.

We arrived at the newish council estate where our suspect resided. Many of the homes had been purchased by the tenants in recent years.

'Next right, Sergeant.' The map was torn from constant use, yet still legible.

'This Jessica's only a few years younger than you, Kimberly. Why don't you take the lead? Feel up to it?'

'Me? You bet, Sergeant. Thanks.'

'Let's keep it low-key. Let her understand the reason we're here. Watch her reactions, her body movements. If necessary, we can return with a search warrant.'

It was early afternoon. Schools

hadn't yet finished so the streets were relatively quiet. The Christmas holidays were almost upon us. There was the occasional tree lit up with coloured bulbs in the dank gardens of the estate. It would be dark within a couple of hours.

'Number sixteen. Slow down. That's it.'

The air was crisp, with the sun low on the horizon. The comforting smells of wood and coal fires permeated the air, reminding me of my childhood in Bromyard.

We donned our overcoats and approached the front door. A black cat darted across cracked flags covered with moss. Good thing I wasn't superstitious. Even so, I felt a sense of apprehension. What were we walking into?

Lights peeked through the drawn curtains. Jessica resided here with her mother and siblings. We pressed the doorbell then, hearing nothing, DS Cameron rattled the letter box cover.

Surprisingly, the door was the plain one that was the sign of a council house throughout the country. Once purchased under the Right-to-Buy scheme, it was generally the first thing the new owners changed.

A flame-haired lady in her forties opened the door.

'What do yer want? Insurance? Double glazing? Well, yer can — '

'Police.' We showed our warrant cards, as I introduced us. 'Mrs Sanderson. We'd like a word with your Jessica. May we come in?'

The look of surprise disappeared. 'Yeah.' Then, in a voice that would put a market trader's to shame, she bellowed up the stairs. 'Jessica. Get yer lazy butt down here. Now. Yer got visitors.'

The bi-fold doors between the living and dining rooms were gone, allowing the oppressive heat from the gas fire to flow everywhere. Toys were scattered on the worn, patterned carpet. A young boy sat at the table colouring a picture.

17

'You officers want a cuppa?'

DS Cameron examined the scene in an instant, noting cracked cups with cigarette butts floating in half-drunk tea.

'Er . . . no thanks, missus. Just had one.'

Jessica bounded down the stairs, entering the room in a fluster. She was skinny, her copper hair tied with an elastic scrunchy. There was a fluffy mauve cardigan on her shoulders, tied loosely around her neck.

At first, the sight of two strangers startled her. Her eyes darted between the sergeant and me. As arranged, I did the introductions, watching her for reactions. She shifted on her bare feet uncomfortably, surreptitiously tossing her cardie over a mobile phone on the coffee table.

From the photo on the mantelpiece, Jessica was the eldest of four children, all with the same ginger hair and freckles as their mother.

'Have you heard the news about the

Bowen girls, Jessica?' I enquired. 'Someone has kidnapped them.'

Her shock appeared genuine.

'Where? When? Are they OK?'

'Last night from their home. The thing is, Jessica, we wondered if you could assist us?'

Mrs Sanderson interrupted.

'Jessie ain't worked there for over a week. Them Bowen people decided they didn't need no help with all that cleaning after all.'

Clearly the teenager hadn't told her mum the real reason for leaving.

'Jessica,' I continued in a gentle voice. 'Do you have any information or idea where the children might be?' DS Cameron watched impassively.

'Me? Course not. I love those munchkins, 'specially Scarlett. I'd never hurt 'em.'

'We didn't suggest you would. But we do need to follow up on any possibilities, especially considering why you left the Bowens'.'

That showed we were aware of the

19

truth. If Mrs Sanderson realised that it wasn't an amicable split, she didn't show it.

I wandered over to her younger brother. There was something I'd noticed.

'That's good.' He glanced up. 'What is it?'

He held it up with a grin. 'A fire engine.'

'It's fantastic. May I look more closely?'

Mrs Sanderson came over.

'Give it to the nice lady, Benny. It can be a present for her.'

'No!' Jessica called out sharply.

It was too late. I had the paper in my hands.

'That's private!' Jessica continued, trying to snatch it. 'You don't have a search warrant.'

'Don't need one, Jessica. Your mother gave it to me.' I showed the drawing to my boss.

'Jess? What's going on? Why yer being so rude?' Mrs Sanderson asked. She must have retrieved the crumpled page from the bin for Benny to draw on, not realising it had been thrown away for a reason.

The paper had a detailed drawing in black marker pen on the reverse. It was a house plan with room labels.

I held it up for all to see before assuming my professional You're-in-deep-trouble voice.

'Miss Jessica Sanderson. This is a floor plan of your former employer's house. Looks like you have some serious explaining to do.'

2

Back at the station, Jessica was very subdued. She'd been advised of her rights and had a court-appointed solicitor with her in the garishly pink interview room.

Some bright spark in headquarters had read that painting the walls pink was proven to calm anyone brought in here. It had only been done two weeks before. I suspected that fuchsia was not the subtle calming shade that was intended, but no one listened to a lowly constable. To men, pink was pink and that was that.

I sat at one side of the desk with DS Cameron by my side. A young female PC stood impassively near the door. A few weeks ago, that had been me. Now I was the one interrogating the suspect.

'I thought it was just for a burglary.

Honest.' Jessica was distraught.

'Start at the beginning, please, Jessica. When were you first contacted?'

She wrung her hands then twisted the cheap, gaudy bracelets around her slim wrists. Her eyes were red from crying. I didn't feel sorry for her, though showing empathy often helped with suspects . . . or so the textbooks said.

'I got a parcel in the post. 'Bout three weeks ago. A phone.'

'This phone?' I interrupted, showing her a mobile in an evidence bag.

'Yeah. There was a note, telling me to ring a number if I wanted two hundred quid. So I did. Some woman told me she wanted a floor plan of the Bowens' place. That was all. I knew it was dodgy, so I refused. You might think I'm a bad person but me Mam taught me principles.'

It seemed Jessica did have some moral standards.

'I held onto the phone. Don't know why.'

'Why did you change your mind?' asked my boss.

Jessica stared down at the table.

'Made me start thinking about the Bowens. They got so much, and me mam struggles all the time to make ends meet. I took a few things . . . little bits to flog at the pawnbrokers. Then Mrs B caught me on camera and sacked me. Just like that. No warning at all.

'Thought I didn't owe her nothing after that. So I rang the number again. I drew the plan a few times 'til I got it right. That one you got was a dud. Then I took it to a café like what the lady on the phone said. Told me some bloke wanted it. She gave me the cash. I gave her the plan.'

'Describe this lady, please,' I prompted.

'Sunglasses, even though it's like middle of winter. A wig. Probably old, 'cause like she had this expensive scarf round her head what covered most of her face.'

'Old,' I said. 'How old?'

'Oh. Thirty. She had leather gloves on too.'

'Did you know her at all?' Steven inquired.

A shake of the head. It seemed like a dead end, just like the man's ring I'd discovered in the girls' room. No identifying features. The inscription was some Army motto yet it was so common, it would lead us nowhere.

'What about her accent?' I pushed, in the vain hope of gleaning some titbit of info.

'Local. And she was white. Also, she kept peering outside into the street. I think she had a friend out there but I never got a good peek at him. He was really tall though.'

Definitely not much to go on. The mobile number had been disconnected. Whoever had paid Jessica had seemingly made certain that if she were caught, she couldn't tell us much.

As we'd had no ransom demand to the mother yet, I decided my DS might be right. He'd suggested this could be some revenge for an unknown slight by the Bowen family. The husband had possibly made enemies in the business world. It was a puzzle, for sure. The longer things went on without any communication, the less good it seemed.

Finally, following more fruitless questions, my DS asked Jessica and her solicitor to stand.

'Jessica Sanderson. I'm charging you with being an accessory to the abduction of Crystal and Scarlett Bowen. Take her away, Constable.'

'What? You're putting me in a cell?' she protested as she was led out. It was upsetting to hear her fear and distress, but she was directly responsible for this nefarious crime. Two loving parents had lost their daughters due to her greed.

Her house plan had enabled the intruders to enter and take the girls. Also, she admitted she'd given them the access code for the alarm, something she'd learned by spying on Candice.

★ ★ ★

The time was after seven when I finished my paperwork. Latest reports from the field told us that the children had not so far been found.

'You go home now, Kimberly,' my boss told me. 'I'll see you Sunday morning.'

I was on leave Saturday after ten days on duty.

'But, Sergeant . . . '

'You have to learn one thing in this job, Kimberly — when to switch off. It's all too easy to let things gnaw away at you if you burn yourself out. You did well today. You were the one who found Jessica and discovered her part in this. Not me. Hopefully we'll make a breakthrough before Sunday — though, if not, I want you back refreshed and ready first thing.'

He was right, of course. Besides, Mum and Dad were expecting me tomorrow.

He was calling it quits too.

'Can I give you a lift home? The wind's quite bitter.'

'It's OK, Sergeant. I just live a few streets away. After today, I could do with some fresh air.'

He nodded sagely. 'Know what you mean, Kimberly. This job, seeing what we see . . . it can get you down. See you Sunday.'

In the locker room, I retrieved my anorak. The walk home was an excuse. Home wasn't worth rushing to. Not since Maisy Jane had moved in.

On the way, I decided to call into Mrs Wu's for some nourishing food. Not as in the five-a-day veg and fruit sense that they were starting to promote on telly. 'Chish and fips' made me feel good . . . that's what I meant by nourishing.

Then again, technically, chips were a vegetable — as were the tomatoes in ketchup.

Chish and fips had been Dad's name for them when we ate out. We'd been so close back then. He'd hummed the

Jaws tune as he lifted his fish with a napkin and made swimming motions.

The Chinese café and takeaway on the corner of my street was a welcome haven on these dark, cold nights. The December wind stung my face, even with my fur-lined hood pulled over my tatty brown hair. It needed a decent shampoo, for sure.

'Hello, Miss Kimberly,' said the wizened older lady as I pushed the door closed behind me. It was too early for the supper-time rush. That suited me fine.

'Hello, Mrs Wu,' I greeted the smiling rosy face of my friend. 'The usual, plus a Coke, please.'

There was a couple holding hands over a table, talking quietly as lovers do. This place had a comforting warmth — and it wasn't simply from the deep fat fryers.

Mrs Wu was one of the first women I'd met since moving into the pre-war semi down the street. I'd never been a fan of cooking for one and, with the

29

irregular hours of a uniformed WPC, I'd found a welcome refuge here. I could hear Mr Wu talking to one of their children in the kitchen, where the mechanical chip cutter chug-chugged away in its rhythmic, hypnotic way.

I took two tartar sauces to place on my tray, electing to eat my cordon-bleu meal in paper rather than use a plasticised plate.

'Sore finger?' she inquired. 'Sorry. I forget. Just sore.'

I admired her efforts at English. Mandarin was so different. She'd tried to teach me a few words but found my pronunciation very amusing. Still, like me, she appreciated the effort to speak another language. I could understand that, to her, 'salt 'n' vinegar' sounded the same as 'sore finger'.

'Yes please. Just salt.' Lately, the smell of vinegar made me nauseous yet here, in this miasma of aromas, I could manage to put up with the occasional whiff of acetic acid.

'Busy day, Miss Kimberly?'

I nodded. 'The two missing children out at Knightsbury Hill.'

'Very sad. Bad people around. Is good they have you to find them.'

I nodded, grateful for her words of support. Truthfully, it wasn't the food I came here for — it was the company.

Eight o'clock. Almost time to go home. Trouble was, number seventeen, Cygnet Place didn't feel like home any more.

There were supposed to be three of us sharing the house. That had changed when Joe moved his girlfriend in, assuming it would be fine with us. It happened little by little until it was clear she was there permanently. Maisy Jane was, in her words, 'between jobs' and showed no signs of wanting to change that.

My other flatmate was Ludavine, a French girl. She had never been any trouble. She, Joe and I worked full-time.

Maisy Jane had spread herself out, single-handedly making it impossible for anyone else to relax in the common areas. The two sitting rooms and our once-tidy kitchen were no-go zones.

A blast of sub-Saharan air struck my face as I entered. The house was like a sauna. I knew MJ felt the cold, yet rather than wear a woolly jumper on her well-endowed body, she insisted on setting the thermostat on twenty-four and lounging around in shirt sleeves.

We'd always split the bills three ways but with Maisy Jane here, the gas and electric had sky-rocketed. Joe was insisting that he shouldn't pay any more as she wasn't using another bedroom.

I went straight to the kitchen with the carton of milk I'd bought. My favourite cup was half-filled with cold coffee and sitting next to some plates covered with furry, stinking food. Maisy had probably found them under their bed and put them downstairs where the washing-up fairy would magically clean them.

I could see sugar spilt everywhere, including the floor. The chocolate on my shelf in the fridge was almost gone, teeth marks and lipstick pointing to the giant rat who'd obviously fancied a snack.

Angrily, I opened the front room door.

'Close it, Kimmy. I've just washed my hair,' Maisy Jane yelled in her fish-wife voice. The telly was on full blast. She was sprawled across the sofa in a nightie and open dressing gown.

'Get out there and clean up the kitchen,' I told her, stopping short of the words I felt like using.

'Sorry. Did you say something about the kitchen, Kimmy? Joe will clean it up when he gets home. I've just done my nails. See.' She showed me her hands. 'Why not watch this video with me? It's a horror movie.'

That cold I'd had a week ago seemingly hadn't completely gone. I wasn't well enough to deal with Maisy Jane tonight. I declined, not so politely. As for seeing something terrifying, I didn't need the TV. The entire house was like a horror movie set.

The bathroom was another disaster zone. Water everywhere, soap on the floor and dirty clothing strewn across the sink and bath.

I picked a bra off the sink and deposited it in the laundry bin, making sure I scrubbed the Maisy Jane germs from my hands. A shower now seemed a better option. At least the cubicle was relatively clean.

Doffing my clothes, I turned on the taps to step into what should have been heavenly bliss. It wasn't. I jumped out just as MJ opened the bathroom door.

'Sorry. Forgot to tell you, Kimmy. No hot water.' Swearing, I struggled to cover myself up.

'No need to use that language, Kimmy. How was I to know you wanted a shower tonight?'

She scurried off back downstairs as I struggled to compose myself. No wonder Ludavine rarely came home except to sleep. This couldn't go on. Our harmonious home where we'd respected one another's space had been turned upside down by Joe's live-in lover and her slovenly nature.

There was nothing more I could do now. At least my bedroom was somewhere I could relax, safe from MJ as it had a lock on the door. I'd grab a shower when I was at Mum's tomorrow.

Right now, it was time to unwind with some Jilly Cooper. My room was quite large so it wasn't claustrophobic, plus it overlooked the tree-studded footpath and the parkland opposite. I'd never brought Barry back here, though, as my single bed was hardly large enough for me.

Going across to close the curtains, I peered outside.

'Oh. Wow.' It had begun to snow. I doubted it would stick — however it was a calming, almost mesmerising spectacle. Fairy-floss snowflakes danced in the tangerine glow of the street lamps.

My anxiety levels dropped instantly,

drawing me back to nights watching snow with Mum and Dad. They called them Winter Wishes — one for every person in the world. They were sent to brighten up the long nights and remind us all of the promise of a wonderful New Year.

Later Joe and Maisy Jane would come upstairs, disturbing my peace with their noisy lovemaking — yet, right now, for a few precious moments, life was as good as it could get.

★   ★   ★

Saturday morning came. I set off for Bromyard as soon as it was light. The snow was gone and there was no black ice, as the cloudy night had kept the temperature above freezing.

No shower, no breakfast — but no early-morning tussle with the washing machine, either. Mum's dryer was preferable to damp clothing basking on the radiators.

It had been years since I moved away

36

from there. It remained my spiritual home; a refuge of familiarity and special memories. The drive took about thirty minutes weaving along twisting roads enclosed by bare hedges of hawthorn.

On impulse I chose to divert via the one-way High Street, past Pettifer's, the local DIY shop that had been there forever. The shops in Bromyard were mostly the same as they had been for years, giving a tranquil familiarity to this town. Even Hereford always seemed to be changing, and not always for the better.

There was a short queue outside the bakery on the top right of the narrow road. I considered stopping for some fresh bread but the thought of being out in the cold put me off. Besides, our family had always been cereal rather than toast people.

I drove back onto the Worcester Road before turning to the right and the newish estate we'd moved to, soon after I'd been born.

'Kimberly. What a surprise,' Mum

said as she opened the door.

'I told you I was coming, Mum.'

'Yes. But you're usually later.' She paused to cough discreetly, before nodding to the two full shopping bags by my feet. 'Washing?'

'Yeah. You don't mind, do you?'

'Of course not.' She pulled her fluffy two-toned dressing gown tighter against the gusting northeasterly wind. 'Come inside to the warmth. Just about to do a cuppa for your dad. He's in bed.'

'I'll do the tea, Mum. I can never suss out that new-fangled washer of yours — buttons and lights everywhere. It'd make a great Christmas tree stuck on the front lawn.'

She coughed once more.

'Besides,' I added, a little concerned, 'policewomen are world famous for brewing up.'

If my mother noticed my sarcastic comment, she didn't react.

'Flu?' I inquired, once we were inside. It felt good to take my bulky coat off.

'I hope not. Had one of those injections — plus my orange juice.' Mum swore by vitamin C for solving the world's diseases. Even though she suffered from asthma, she was usually fit as a flea — without the need to jump around a lot.

While she busied herself with the *Star Wars* style washer, I filled three mugs.

'Could you take his highness' tea upstairs, Kimberly? Feeling a bit weak at the moment.'

I assumed it was her attempt to get us talking.

'If I must. Don't think Dad'll appreciate seeing me this early.' I looked down at the *Mr Grumpy* cup I'd bought him as a joke. It wasn't so funny now.

She gave me a hug. 'He'll love to see you, baby. He does care about you. It's just . . . '

Her voice trailed off. We'd had this conversation before too many times.

Inspecting the kitchen, it appeared

to have lost its usual immaculate showhome appearance. Was Mum struggling? It wasn't as though she was that old. She was fifty . . . no, fifty-one.

'Go on up. Say hello. I hate it when you two fight.'

To be fair, we never fought in the true sense of the word; it was more an uneasy truce. Me talking about work was a no-no, that was all.

'Sure, Mum. I'll try.'

Once at the top of the stairs, I called out.

'Dad? I have your tea.'

At first there was no answer so I called again.

'Dad? Are you decent?'

There was a pause.

'Kimberly? Am I decent, did you say? Well, I'm wearing that dreadful dressing gown you gave me last birthday but apart from that . . . '

I pushed the door ajar. He was sitting up with a Tom Clancy novel in his hands. An open newspaper was on the duvet on Mum's side.

'How are you?'

'Depends, Kimberly. You still a copper?'

'Don't start, Dad. Actually, I've been working on an important case.'

I mentally kicked myself for mentioning work.

'Not that kidnapping thingy over Knightsbury Hill way?'

I almost dropped his mug. There was a news blackout on the case. What was going on?

My father must have noticed my shock.

'What? Don't tell me you don't know about the ransom demand? Some copper you are.'

'Ransom . . . but . . . ' Although his last words had hurt me, I was damned if I'd give him the satisfaction of showing it.

'On the radio. The kidnappers sent letters to all the media. Your precious force seems to be incapable of doing anything about it.'

41

That was the last straw.

'Don't you preach to me, Father. I was there comforting those girls' poor mother yesterday. Clearly there were developments after I left last night, but I was one of those 'useless coppers' out there trying to find those kiddies while you sat in your comfy, warm office, ready to pass judgment on us. It was me who tracked down one of the women involved. Me . . . So just keep your damned opinions to yourself.'

I put his cup down, angrily, sloshing some milky tea onto the bedside table. I didn't care. Closing the door with a slam, I marched down the stairs, fuming that I'd let him get to me yet again.

Behind me, I heard a pleading apology. It was too late.

Mum was waiting. 'That was a record. Less than five minutes. I was . . . sort of hopi . . . '

She burst into a coughing fit, doubled over as she struggled for breath. I rushed to give her some water.

'Are you certain you don't need the doctor? That cough sounds pretty rough.'

'A doctor? Goodness me, no. It's just a winter cold.' Then, as if deciding a distraction might work, she perked up. 'Guess who's dropping by later?'

I grinned. 'Hmm. Let's see . . . Begins with M and ends with K.'

Mum nodded, smiling. Mark had been my friend since secondary school. He was living locally in a two-bed apartment.

The mobile computer business he'd begun last year was doing well. The hands-on repairs had lately given way to a consultancy role. Computers seemed to be the latest thing for some businesses, though most folk didn't have much idea how to make the best use of them.

Not that he'd convinced me or my parents to splash out on a tower box, floppy discs and bulky glorified telly screen. Not yet, anyway. There was a perfectly good Amstrad 464 in the attic.

What did anyone ordinary need one of these things for anyway?

I did remember him saying that everyone's life would change once they had new windows in the system, to which my mum suggested they should buy new curtains as well. Mark had laughed as though it was something amusing.

'Trust me, Kimberly,' he'd told me last week. 'This will transform all our lives — and those of our children too.'

As if. It was just the latest fad — just like those Intellivision games I used to play with Dad in the Eighties.

Then Mum shocked me with a statement out of the blue.

'I think Mark's sweet on you, Kimberly.'

'Mark? No way. We're mates. Anyway, I've got Barry in my life.' I paused, wondering. 'What makes you believe that?'

My mother took a moment to catch her breath. 'He . . . he makes special trips to visit us, whenever you're here.

Also, I've noticed the change in his expression whenever you mention Barry. He tries to cover it up. I think he's jealous.'

I'd had a few boyfriends over the years, though my relationship with Barry was more serious.

'He's never told me he fancies me,' I pointed out. It was probably Mum and her fascination with all those romance stories she enjoyed. She'd never met Barry, so she was probably reading more into my friendship with my old friend. Wishful thinking, maybe?

She had kept mentioning that I was getting on a bit, even though I was only in my mid-twenties. And there were those not-so-subtle comments about my two best friends now being married and pregnant.

Mark was bright, I had to concede that. However, he was shy and lacked confidence as well as being one of those guys with two left feet, no use at any sports.

By contrast, I had been a fit athlete

all through school. As for his looks, he was OK but I preferred men of the tall, dark and handsome variety.

'Mark and me? It'll never happen, Mum. Not unless either he or I have a personality transplant.'

★ ★ ★

By the time I'd had my delicious hot shower and dried my hair, Dad was up and dressed. It was a strained yet polite time until Mark arrived around ten-twenty.

Mark was a little taller than I was, about five foot ten. He was lean rather than skinny. Buddy Holly glasses and hair the colour of milky tea, long and untidy, completed the ensemble. Tall, dark and handsome he definitely wasn't.

To be fair, he was a breath of fresh air in the sombre atmosphere; bubbly and with a definite opinion when he did overcome that inherent shyness. Not that his opinion often made much sense. He seemed to think on a different wavelength to the rest of us and as for his sense of humour, let's just say it was an acquired taste.

His strengths lay in electronics and computers, both software and hardware, whatever they were. At school he was one of those people you hated in Maths, able to give the square root of two hundred and eighty-three in seconds. Most of us struggled to understand what a square root was.

Now with his so-called computer skills, he wasn't going to change the world. Games like *Space Invaders* were for kids, and the concept of us normal people sending letters to one another by computer . . . that was totally unbelievable.

Even Dad wanted Mark involved in his attempt to apologise for his earlier insults to me.

'Mark. Have you heard Kimberly's involved with that abduction of the twins? Impressive stuff. Caught one of the culprits, she did.' He smiled at me uncomfortably, although I did appreciate his effort, and put my hand on his arm.

'They're not twins — just sisters,' I pointed out.

'Well done,' Mark said, pushing his glasses up. He always did that when he was nervous. 'Actually . . . I might start seeing you at the station. I've been asked to do some consultancy work, upgrading their IT department.'

He noticed our blank looks and elaborated.

'IT? Information Technology. Lots of new words. Most of the police systems are so antiquated, I half expect to see an abacus alongside the Amstrads and word processors.'

I was pleased for Mark and told him so. Nevertheless, something was bothering me about what my father had said earlier. It was time to meet him half way.

'Dad. How did the news of the kidnapping leak out?'

'Don't know. Just heard it on the

news. Maybe there's something in the morning paper?'

He went upstairs to retrieve it. Normally his interest in the paper was confined to the sports pages — West Brom or Birmingham City.

'Here. Page two.' He shoved the paper at us and I read the article aloud. Mum came over to listen.

The facts were all there in black and white. There was also a coloured photo of the sisters cowering in some room, half-eaten sandwiches on a plate in front of them. The look of fear on their little faces was heart-wrenching.

'*There was a letter, delivered by Yahoo mail, to the newspaper offices yesterday. The kidnappers sent it and the photo.*' I put the paper down.

'That doesn't make sense,' my dad and I declared simultaneously.

I was aware that he was an avid reader of real crime stories. Perhaps being aware of that seedier side of life was one reasons he was so opposed to my being in the police.

In any case, I respected his opinion. Like me, he'd be aware that abductors usually kept a low profile, expressly forbidding victims to contact the media or police. These ones were apparently intent on broadcasting their crime for everyone to see. Was it bravado, or something more?

'This is a distraction. It must be,' Dad surmised, reading on. 'They're treating it as a game between them and the police — and you, Kimberly, are one of the pawns.' He pointed to a quote from the criminal's computer letter. There it was; my name and that of my boss as investigating officers. How could they have possibly learned that?

Our heated discussion was interrupted by Mum going into another coughing fit. I went to her.

'Why not go back to bed? I'll do you a hot toddy. You need to take it easy.'

Helping her upstairs, I appreciated how weak she was. The bedroom didn't have any heaters on. Considering that she had a temperature, I thought that was better as I tucked her into bed.

If it were a cold, it was a bad one. A few minutes later, I came back with a hot drink of brandy, lemon and sugar. It was the way she liked it on the few occasions she'd been ill before.

When I went downstairs, I found Dad and Mark in the lounge. The comfy three-piece suite was still there, showing signs of wear on the arms — as well as my clumsy attempts at experimenting with nail polish when I was a girl.

'How is she? Your mother?' Dad enquired, obviously concerned.

'Not great.'

'She insisted on getting up this morning. Wanted to tidy up before you came, she did. I told her it didn't matter but you know your mum. 'After all. It's only Kimberly,' I said.'

I grinned. It used to be one of his catchphrases, a joke in our close-knit family. Where had it all gone wrong?

'I'll sort out the kitchen later,' I suggested.

'We could do it together, Kimberly. For your mum. She'll hate us interfering though, especially if we mix up those darn spice jars of hers.'

The house was Mum's domain. Dad's role was to go out and earn the money, running the small metal fabrication plant by the church car park. It was one of those old-fashioned traditional marriages that worked for them.

I doubted I'd ever be a contented housewife — domestic bliss was the furthest thing from my mind. This new job was far more important than choosing matching tea towels.

'What else does the paper tell us?' I prompted my fellow detectives, as I took a sip of fresh coffee which I'd brought in for us all.

'Doesn't say a lot more. I believe that whoever did this wants to humiliate the police as well as putting the parents through hell. There's a lot of vindictive hatred here. In fact, I'm not even certain that ransom is the real motive.'

Dad sat back, scrutinising the photo while rubbing the greying stubble on his chin. Saturdays had always been a lazy day for him.

Mark produced a magnifying glass from the desk drawer.

'But the photo is for proof of life. See the newspaper cutting on the wall? It's yesterday's. That's what a kidnapper would show when asking for a ransom. Everyone knows that.'

'Exactly,' Dad added. 'But they haven't made any ransom demands yet. None. Doesn't make sense at all. It's like they're playing silly beggars with everyone.'

At that moment, Mark's mobile phone rang. I had one too, though my father was stuck in the past. He even had a *Magnum*-type moustache. He and my new boss had a lot in common.

'Yes. Speaking . . . Slow down, Terry . . . They what? All of them? I'll be thirty minutes. Don't, I repeat, don't touch them until I arrive.'

He listened for a few more seconds, his face blanching in spite of the heat in the room. He was clearly upset.

'Sorry, guys. I have to go. That was the duty officer at your headquarters. All six of the police computers have crashed. Some sort of virus attack.'

As he struggled into his overcoat and took out his keys, he turned to my father.

'A distraction for something bigger, you suggested. You were dead right. The kidnappers sent a Yahoo mail to HQ just as they promised they would. Because the police thought it was the ransom note that they were expecting, things were rushed. The virus checks that I'd set up were ignored. There was no demand for money — only a cheeky animation saying *BOOM!* before everything went dead throughout Hereford HQ. Now there's chaos and it's up to me to repair it all . . . if I can.'

In the porch, Mark asked me to come to the car. I slipped on my boots and coat, putting the latch on.

'What's going on, Mark? I've not seen you this agitated since Tommy Nolan broke your specs in Science in fourth year.'

He examined the other homes in our quiet cul-de-sac, searching for I don't know what. Then he held me closely so he could whisper in my ear.

'That electronic message said something worrying. There were threats against you and your Detective Sergeant Cameron by name, saying you should watch your backs.'

I gasped. It was clear that arresting Jessica Sanderson had upset the criminals.

'You'd best keep an eye out, Kimberly. Someone is feeding them information . . . possibly some person in the force itself.'

I gave him a reassuring smile, trying to mask my own apprehensions. He hugged me closely before kissing me on the cheek. He'd never kissed me in all the years we'd been together.

'Blinking hell, mister. Now you're

really scaring me' I joked. Then I mentioned a thought I'd had.

'It's a shame this kidnapper didn't use a proper letter. You know, with a stamp on it? We might track him down from the postmark — see whereabouts he'd sent it from, at least.'

Mark examined my face. He was wondering about what I'd suggested then his eyes opened wide.

'You're a genius, Kimberly. Why didn't I think about it?'

'Think about what?' It was great to be called a genius yet it would be even better to be told why.

He removed those horrid glasses of his to rub his eyes.

'Electronic mail does have a post-mark on it, to tell other computers where it came from. It's called an IP address . . . Internet Protocol. There's a series of numbers that I can track down to wherever this so-and-so forwarded the mail from. If he's not all that up to date with computers he might not realise that, so we can find him — and

56

hopefully the missing girls. As I said, Kimberly, you are smart as well as beautiful . . . er, didn't mean to say that.'

It was a little embarrassing. In his excitement, my best friend had disclosed another side of himself. Neither of us spoke for a moment. Finally, he put his glasses on and faced his car.

'Just be careful. Bye,' he called over his shoulder, not daring to look me in the eye.

I watched as he went to his old Vauxhall Cavalier and drove away before heading back up the cobbled path.

Jeez, Mark, I thought. *Talk about complicating matters.*

There was a noise behind me. Another car started up further down the street. I didn't recognise it. At that moment, I felt a sudden chill. Unfortunately, it had nothing to do with the wintry weather.

3

Once inside again, I phoned my DS to check if I should come in. He explained, quite firmly, that I shouldn't. He was already aware of the friendship between Mark and me. It had been disclosed on the agreement Mark had signed regarding confidentiality when he'd accepted the consultancy position.

Dad and I then set to, cleaning the kitchen and making lunch for the three of us.

Mum said she'd managed some sleep when I took her food upstairs. Being Mum, it was difficult to tell if she was simply telling me what I wanted to hear. The toddy probably did make her drowsy.

Her chesty cough was more subdued though it was raspier. Her temperature was lower.

Alone with Dad, it was time for one

of those father/daughter talks that was long overdue. We'd been skirting around the issue for too long.

I started off.

'It's those books you've been reading these past few years, isn't it? You always loved thrillers yet now you only read real-life crime accounts.'

He sighed before squeezing my hand.

'Not any longer, love. I've chucked them out. Last week. Now I'm back to Tom Clancy and Alistair MacLean. Might even look at Stephen King. At least they're all make-believe, they are.'

I recalled the novel I'd seen him reading this morning, *Raise The Titanic*. I'd seen the movie but it wasn't my style. On the other hand, Dad had always been into Boys' Own adventures as a kid. That spaceman Dan Dare was his favourite.

'It was eating me up, knowing that you had to deal with actual villains like in those Real Crime books. All my life I've protected you from the seedier side. I felt so helpless when you joined the force. Reading crime novels and magazines was like an addiction. It really was. I knew it was making me worse and I was taking it out on you.'

It made sense.

'What prompted you to give it up?'

'Mark, believe it or not. He'd met an ex-copper in his job, one that was involved in a few of the cases I'd read about. Mark introduced us and we spent a lot of time talking. Although he'd retired before you joined, he'd worked at New Scotland Yard. He was a real-life Sweeney. In any case, he explained those real crime stories were as fictitious as any of the thrillers I read, and real policing wasn't as bad as the magazines made out.'

If Dad had asked me, I'd have told him the same thing. Now I had a question for him.

'Why were you so anti-police this morning? You really kicked off.'

He chuckled.

'Yeah, I did. Sorry about that. The

truth is . . . it's a bit embarrassing, kitten . . . You woke me up from a really good dream. I'd nodded off while reading. Getting old, I guess. I'm not a morning person these days. I did try to apologise but . . . '

'I'd already stormed out. Guess I inherited your grumpy genes. All this time I thought you objected to the police not being good enough for me when you were simply concerned for my well-being.'

I gave him a warm smile before continuing.

'I'm not that young pushover who was bullied by Jenny Nicholson. These days, I can look after myself. Been doing martial arts training for years. As for Jenny, I met her a few months ago. She hadn't changed. Nowadays I'm three inches taller than her, not the other way around. She'd been caught shoplifting.'

Dad sat forward on the settee, looking up the stairs as he wondered about Mum.

'Did she recognise you?'

'Not at first. When she did, she made some disparaging statements before trying to attack me. Don't worry, Dad. She didn't come close. My colleague restrained her and instead of a community order, she's doing jail time for resisting arrest. What goes around, comes around.'

* * *

I left my parents' around three-thirty. Mum had come down to afternoon tea which Dad and I had prepared together. She was better, though we were both concerned for her.

I wanted to avoid the hedge-shrouded winding roads at night. It was dusk when I drove up Cygnet Place to park outside my rented lodgings.

Inside, I made a point of avoiding Maisy Jane. She had the radio on full blast as usual. It was terrible to feel so ill-at-ease in my own place.

At least I'd be out for dinner. Barry

was collecting me at seven. I was looking forward to our Saturday night together. Taking no chances with the couch-potato-from-hell using the hot water, I decided to shower straight away. Twice in a day wasn't unusual for me. Besides, I was still chilly from the drive back as my car heater wasn't working very well.

Half way through, MJ knocked on the bathroom door. I'd locked it this time.

'You still in there, Kimberly? It's time for my shower. I need to make myself beautiful.'

I felt like suggesting a paper bag on her head would be better than a shower if that was her aim. Then I chastised myself for being so mean.

'Just another hour, Maisy Jane. Two at the most,' I shouted back, pleased when I heard her stomp off down the stairs.

'There. That'll learn you,' I muttered, parroting her favourite mangled English expression.

Although I wasn't normally vindictive, people like Jenny and Maisy Jane brought out the something-that-rhymes-with-witch in me.

Later, as I was struggling into my tight slacks and my favourite burgundy blouse, MJ's dulcet tones reverberated throughout the house. Apparently, there was no hot water. As Ludavine would have said, 'Quelle dommage!' which simply meant 'What a shame'.

Barry came by just before seven. He was dressed more casually than me, wearing gloves and a warm beige overcoat. The multi-coloured pom-pom knitted hat didn't match the ensemble though I could understand his rationale; his coffee-brown hair was cropped close to his head.

He'd rung the front bell. After peering through the bedroom window to see his Volvo coupé, I locked my door and hurried down the stairs, narrowly missing stepping on MJ's hair dryer.

Barry would never come inside. His parents were well-off and had bought him his own flat, so he didn't need to watch his pennies like us mere mortals. The way things were going in my house, I could see the appeal.

He gave me a cursory kiss. 'Hurry up, Kimberly. I'm freezing out here.'

There wasn't any *Oh, you look great* or *Love that perfume.* That wasn't my Barry's way.

In the car he turned the hot air full-on. The heated seats made it doubly oppressive. When I complained about the warmth blowing on my face, he turned it down, but just a smidgen.

Conversation was an endless description about the stag party for his brother the previous night. I'd never met him. In fact, I'd never met any of his family, apart from some aunt that we came across by accident at the movies one night. That was short and sweet; Barry was in a rush.

I tolerated this one-sided conversation for as long as I could, finally asking if he'd heard about the missing children.

'Course I have. This Lollipop Man is making a laughing stock of the police investigation. Don't tell me you're involved in that fiasco?'

First Dad. Now my boyfriend. At least Dad had his reasons and we'd worked through that. I ignored Barry's stupid question.

'Lollipop Man?'

'It's what he calls himself. Heard it on the radio before I came out for you.'

I was surprised at the arrogance of this criminal, taking his name from those men and women who helped children.

I turned my gaze to Barry, his features silhouetted and eerily lit by street lights as he drove. Why did I love this man when he showed such contempt for my profession? It wasn't as though he was faultless himself. Only last week he'd mentioned that he'd ruined a new boiler he was installing, adding that his dad, who owned the company, wasn't very pleased.

'Hey. In spite of what you've heard,

66

the police are doing their best to solve this case. Next time think before you open your mouth.'

Immediately he reacted, realising he'd overstepped the mark.

'Sorry sweetheart, I don't know the facts and I wasn't thinking straight. Probably had too many drinks last night. I don't want us to fall out. You mean so much to me. Am I forgiven?'

I let him stew for some moments before I put my hand on his.

'OK. Let's go to Dalmonico's for dinner to celebrate us being friends again. It's a bit more expensive but I do so love their desserts.'

I saw him lose that toothy smile of his for an instant. I was always going to forgive him — but why not take advantage of the situation? It wasn't as though he was short of money. His parents saw to that.

'Yeah. Sure. Whatever you want, sweetie. Dalmonico's it is.'

★　★　★

67

It was a mixed night. The food was superb as always, but Barry wasn't.

He'd begun by making some inane comment, wondering if kidnapping was so-called because kids were taken from their parents and that there should be a new word, adultnapping, for older victims. It all went downhill from there.

'Guess who I bumped into at the stag do? . . . Alison.'

I almost choked on my salmon tagliatelle.

'Your ex?'

'The one and only. She was so amazing. Lost weight too. Did I tell you about when we first met?' He spent the next forty-odd minutes describing his 'one true love' and all that they'd shared together, finally concluding with 'It's such a pity that you're not more like her, Kimberly. Then we could really have something special.'

If there were prizes for the most insensitive reminiscences by a man, Barry would have won first, second and third prizes quite convincingly.

The evening finished with him suggesting we return to his place for the night and me saying no.

He gave me a lift back to my place, even though he was far from happy.

'I've an early start tomorrow,' I explained, trying not to show how angry I was. I considered dumping him — however tonight had been a one-off as he was normally very considerate and loving.

★   ★   ★

On Sunday morning, I arrived at the station early. It was important to catch up on the latest developments. DS Cameron wasn't pleased. Apparently, we were no closer to finding the girls.

'There's a briefing in ten minutes, Kimberly. Good to have you back.' I could see the concern in his eyes. This case had taken on a much more intense meaning for him as well.

Right on time DCI Aldershot entered

the room. He was the Senior Investigating Officer. It was still dark outside.

We were appraised of the latest news. The Lollipop Man has been busy, announcing to the media that he'd acted to save the children by taking them from their cruel and abusive parents. It was all rubbish of course — clear from his previous requests that a ransom be paid.

I recalled Dad's assessment; that it was a distraction. Lollipop Man was proclaiming that he was some do-gooder Robin Hood. Sadly, I believed that some of the locals might believe his fantasy, admiring him as a hero.

The DCI then introduced my friend, Mark. I felt a touch of pride and was grateful that his skills were aiding our own intensive efforts to track the perpetrator down. Admittedly the jacket he was wearing was too large, and Paisley ties belonged back in the era of Flower Power.

Although clearly nervous to be

addressing our group, Mark explained the situation concisely. Even those of us who weren't computer literate were able to follow events.

'The virus that infected all the computer network has now been quarantined, and Windows 95 is running once more. I've installed anti-virus software and a sort of barrier called a firewall to prevent what is referred to as hacking by this person.'

He then nodded in my direction.

'Thanks to a . . . suggestion by DC Frost, the tech guys and I have been able to trace the infected communication back to the place it was sent from. Officers are raiding it . . . ' he checked his watch, 'right about now.'

'Where is it, Mark?' I realised I might have spoken out of turn and blushed.

'Ludlow. It's about half an hour from here, I think.' I realised he didn't know Hereford very well as we'd spent our school days in Bromyard and generally went to Worcester for big shops.

The DCI agreed, adding that, as

Ludlow was in Shropshire, police there were also involved.

'Cross-county co-operation, ladies and gentlemen. Our priority is the safe return of the lasses.' Occasionally his Yorkshire upbringing seeped through in his speech.

'As to the media, they won't be directly printing or broadcasting any more of these outlandish letters from him. I had to make it clear to the papers and such that to do so might lead to repercussions as they were impeding our investigation.'

'Repercussions, sir?' a young uniformed bobby asked.

DCI Aldershot gave a sardonic smile, visible though his neatly trimmed black beard. He reminded me of pictures of Long John Silver.

We knew the DCI was a hard man when the situation called for it. A day or two in the cells wasn't out of the question if the editors didn't play ball.

It was DS Cameron's turn to speak.

'We're positive that the news of

Jessica Sanderson's detention wasn't leaked by anyone here. That points to the only other person who knew — her mother. Somehow, she contacted this Lollipop Man, telling him of the visit by DC Frost and yours truly. It also explains how the crim knew our names to tell everyone. On that assumption, the two of us will revisit her this morning.'

'Thanks, Steven. We're still awaiting news of this ransom, though I'm beginning to think it's a red herring. Nothing this LM does is predictable.'

It was the first time anyone had abbreviated the daft name this master-mind insisted on calling himself. I suggested we use this sobriquet instead and it was agreed. 'Lollipop Man' felt totally wrong for such a sinister villain.

The DCI explained to us that Mr Bowen, the girls' father, was snowed in. There were no flights out of Bonn for an expected two days, plus train tracks and main roads were impassable. Our liaison officer remained with Mrs

Bowen, who was very distraught. An old school friend had volunteered to stay with her. It was good to hear she had someone else to support her.

Just before we were dismissed, I recalled an inconsistency I'd noticed and raised a hand.

'Excuse me, sir. I thought that yesterday's electronic mail was about the ransom — yet you said we're still waiting to hear?'

'DC Frost . . . Kimberly . . . It was simply a ruse to infect our systems. There was nothing else there. I do a bit of fishing on my many days off — ' There was some quiet laughter as we all knew he was a workaholic. 'He used the same principle. Entice the fish with a wriggling worm on a hook then reel it in. The ransom note was the worm and we fell for his ruse, literally hook, line and sinker.

'LM doesn't play by the rules. With him you have to expect the unexpected. He could be watching us at any time. So, final words. Keep alert everyone, especially you two, DS Cameron and DC Frost. He seems to have singled you out to play his games with for some bizarre reason.'

★ ★ ★

With my boss driving, I had a chance to digest the latest information. It wasn't pleasant to be targeted by some evil criminal.

Prior to leaving, I'd done some checks on Mrs Sanderson. She didn't have a landline phone due to previous non-payment of some hefty bills to British Telecom. The search warrant we'd obtained on Friday was still current, and encompassed the entire property rather than Jessica's possessions alone. The forensics team hadn't discovered any connection to LM apart from the pay-as-you-go untraceable phone that Jessica had used to contact him. The number she'd dialled was now disconnected. No surprise there.

Mrs Sanderson opened the door and

75

immediately begin a tirade.

'You two again. When yer letting Jessie go?'

'Let's put it this way, Mrs Sanderson. I wouldn't wait up for her. She's in serious trouble. May we come in? Or would you prefer to come with us to the station while we search your house once more?'

My boss wasn't a happy bunny and Mrs Sanderson realised that. She grudgingly allowed us to enter.

'Love what you've done to the place. You've obviously been busy, cleaning and all,' he added sarcastically.

The state of the rooms was even worse than the other day. Dirty dishes filled the sink while take-away cartons and beer cars nestled between overflowing ashtrays. This was one of those houses where you wiped your feet on the way out.

I donned some plastic gloves, as much for my health as for not contaminating any evidence. The toddler, Benny, was nowhere to be seen.

When Steven launched into his questioning, I searched for the item I was certain would incriminate her. She probably had it well hidden by the time the forensics team first arrived after we arrested Jessica, and took her phone away. How could we have guessed there were two untraceable phones in the house?

It didn't take long. She'd never expected us to return so she'd put it in the most convenient place . . . her handbag. Taped to the back was another number with the words *If the coppers come round, phone me.*

Returning to my boss, I brandished it for the lady to see. 'Guess what I found? It looks like you've only used it once — immediately after we arrested Jessica.'

Steve cautioned her.

'Can't prove nothing, coppers. Anyways it's mine. Yer can check.'

I answered, watching her belligerent attitude evaporate in a flash. 'Already did. You don't have a mobile. I put it to you that you used it to tell the kidnappers what happened — along with our names.'

She sighed. 'What if I did? No law against talking. 'Sides, he paid me good money, just like my Jess.'

I popped the bulky mobile phone into an evidence bag before taking her by the elbow.

'I think it's time for a family reunion. What do you think, Detective Sergeant? Adjoining cells with a view?'

The lack of any noise or other voices struck me all of a sudden. It was Sunday morning.

'Where are the children? We'll need to notify social.'

Mrs Sanderson spat on her already mucky carpet. 'They took 'em already. Yesterday.'

As Steve called for a marked car to take her in, I checked with the out-of-hours council number. Mrs Sanderson was telling the truth for once. She had a long history of child neglect.

Steven held up the evidence bag. 'Maybe your boyfriend can trace the number she called before it's turned off like Jessica's. I'm not holding my breath, though. This guy seems to be like a magician, always with a few tricks up his sleeve.'

'Mark's not my boyfriend. He's an old mate from school days, that's all. What on earth makes you think we're romantically attached?'

My own mobile buzzed before Steven could answer.

'Excuse me while I check this.' I pressed connect. 'Hello.' At the same time, I half noticed a police car arrive at the end of the drive where we were waiting.

'That you, Kimberly?' a male voice replied. 'Didn't know if this was the right number.'

My father never rang me. Something was wrong. 'Dad?'

'It's your mother, kitten,' he began. 'She's been taken to hospital. That cough . . . ' He took a breath to compose himself. 'She's better but her chest was so bad, breathing and all, I called the ambulance this morning, I did. Doctor's suspected bronchitis rather than that 'flu bug that's going around. She sends her love. They're pumping stuff into her ... inta something antibiotics.'

'Intravenous?'

'Yeah. What you said.'

I turned to Steven who had just placed Mrs Sanderson in the marked police car.

'It's my mother. They've taken her to hospital. Could you drop me off?'

'Absolutely, Kimberly. It's on the way back anyway. I can interview our latest prisoner by myself.' He opened the car door for me showing a touch of old-fashioned gallantry.

'I'm on my way, Dad,' I explained before disconnecting the call. My pulse was racing from the news. Mum had suffered from bronchitis before, and I kicked myself for not being more vigilant yesterday.

The trip was a few minutes, yet it seemed to take ages. Inside the hospital, I hurried to the ward Mum was in, breathing a sigh of relief when I saw her sitting up in bed. She had nasal tubes connected to the oxygen input on the wall. My father was holding her hand, rabbiting on as he often did when he was anxious or uptight.

'Told you not to panic, kitten,' he said, noting my expression. 'But it's good to see you here, it is.'

I gave Mum a kiss along with a heart-felt cuddle. Her coughing appeared less frequent, but her skin was almost as pale as the starchy sheets.

'Said they want me to stay for a few days, Kimberly. The asthma compli-cates matters, is what the nice young doctor told me.'

Studying the nursing staff and white-coated men and women who were busy with female patients on this ward, gave me a sense of comfort.

She was in the best place for care. I stayed for just under an hour until DS

Cameron arrived. He'd phoned earlier to check on the situation. After introductions, he asked if I wanted to stay or go with him to the Bowens' residence.

My parents said to go.

'Those two nippers need all the help they can get, Kimberly. They really do,' Dad stated.

Leaving with Steve, he brought me up to speed. Tracking down the sender of the electronic mail yesterday and the day before in Ludlow hadn't yielded any positive results. They'd been dispatched from a place called an internet café. No one there recalled who was using the computer in question either time, and payment wasn't made by Visa or Mastercard, or by cheque. It had been a wild goose chase yet it had to be done. Somewhere the mysterious LM would slip up and then my police colleagues would find Crystal and Scarlett.

★ ★ ★

At the Bowens', we were greeted by a woman I didn't recognise. She was wearing denims with a man's shirt.

We could hear reporters by the gates which fronted the long elm-sided driveway to the turning circle where we'd parked.

'Police? Hi. I'm Rhonda . . . Rhonda Whiting.'

'Candice's friend from school?' I guessed.

She smiled. 'Yep. That's me. I've just arrived here myself. Come on in.'

Rhonda appeared pleasant enough, offering to take our coats. She had one of those happy faces that instantly brightened up the sombre mood. We slipped our shoes off in deference to the beige carpet. Steven had a hole in the toe of his thick socks. I grinned as my boss apologised.

'I expect my own kids will give me some more pairs for Christmas. It's a family tradition.' Then he added for my benefit, 'Just hope they don't give me bright orange ones again this time.'

Rhonda ambled ahead of us, her long, blonde pony-tail swishing from side to side. She twisted her head towards us as she passed the kitchen.

'Candy's husband is struggling to get back. When I heard about the terrible thing that had happened, I offered to come over and stay. The poor dear. It was the least I could do.'

I hoped her being here would help. It must have been horrible for Candice having no one to share the grief she must be feeling.

Rhonda explained that Mrs Bowen was on the phone to her parents. Seeing us, Candice looked over hopefully. Steven shook his head, sadly.

'The police are here. No news,' she said on the phone. 'I'll call you back later, Mummy.'

Candice was surprised and saddened to hear of Jessica's betrayal when we explained the latest.

'I cannot believe she could be that vindictive, DS Cameron. Goes to show how you don't really know people, even when you think you do. She was so doting with the girls.'

All during this conversation, I had a sense that something felt wrong — not with the others, but with myself. Maybe I'd caught Mum's cough — yet it didn't feel like the usual cold or flu symptoms. It was necessary to concentrate to take in Steven's words.

He must have noticed my vagueness.

'You okay, Kimberly? Your eyes . . . '

'Maybe a glass of water, please?' I requested, uncomfortable at the attention. When Rhonda handed it to me, I accidentally knocked it, spilling some on the table.

'No worries,' Rhonda announced. 'I'll get a sponge from the laundry.' She returned with a cloth almost straight away. No damage was done except to my self-esteem.

As we stood to leave, Steven explained we had other leads to pursue, both from our own investigations and from the massive public response to our request for assistance. Sightings of the girls everywhere from Brighton to Oldham were coming in. Seemingly it was big news.

'The kidnapper's blatant arrogance has enraged people out there, Mrs Bowen. You have a lot of support. Like all criminals, he's not infallible and must have made mistakes. We'll track him down; little Crystal and Scarlett too. You have my word on that.'

It was a heartfelt statement to make. Unhappily, I wondered if he were making a promise which he might not be able to keep.

★ ★ ★

Back at the station, I continued to feel a bit off-colour. The drive had been uncomfortable. It was as though the summer sunlight had reappeared in the midst of December. It was necessary to squint almost the entire time.

Making our way to the incident room, Steven spied a visitor.

'Wait up, Doc. Just the guy I want.'

He stopped the older man, shaking his hand and clapping him on the shoulder. 'Kimberly here is a bit queasy. Wonder if you could give her a quick once-over?'

Doctor Little checked his watch. He was the on-call doctor for staff and the occasional prisoner complaining of a dodgy tummy from meals we ordered in from the local take-away.

'Actually, I was on my way home. Couldn't her own doctor examine her?'

It was a weak excuse and I protested.

'I'm registered in Bromyard. Not seen anyone in six years. And I'm living nearby these days.'

He was known as Dr Dolittle by my colleagues and was not one of the hardest workers in the NHS. Checking his watch yet again, he stroked his designer-stubble and relented.

'Somewhere private please,' I requested when he removed a stethoscope from his battered Glad-stone bag. 'Or do you expect me to strip off in front of the entire shift?'

'Bolshie girl, aren't you?' he muttered with a grudging smile at the fuss I was making. I kept my arms folded across my chest. 'OK. Follow me.'

We found a suitable office where he closed the Venetian blinds and door. Steven hovered protectively outside.

'What's the problem, DC Frost? That time of the month?'

I glared at him.

'My apologies. Out of order. Long day. Shall I start again?'

Gradually, I relaxed before describing the strange unease I was feeling. The more rapid blinking was something he commented on. He shone a desk lamp into my eyes but I winced, asking him to turn it off.

'Let's try again with a flashlight, please,' he suggested, opening his bag. This time was less painful. He rubbed his chin, thoughtfully.

'Your left pupil isn't reacting in the same way as your right. Unusual. Have you had any recent infections?'

'Bit of a sniffle. That's all. What is it?'

'Nothing to be alarmed about by itself. I suspect it's the beginning of . . . well, I'd rather not speculate. We'll have to wait and see what develops. Equally, it might fix itself overnight. Our bodies are marvellous things for self-repair. Tell you what, I'll make an appointment first thing at my group practice. Nine-thirty. I'll squeeze you in. If you feel better, just cancel. If it becomes worse, give us a bell tonight. I'll be on this number till seven-thirty.'

Dr Little gave me a business card before smiling reassuringly.

'Probably nothing, although you should take the rest of the day off. I'll sort out a sick note.'

It was a difficult decision on my part to accept. There was so much to do in tracking down the girls.

'I'm on a case.'

Dr Little sealed it with a firm, 'Don't argue, young lady. Doctor's orders.'

Absolutely blinking great, I thought. Asking if I could visit Mum, he advised against it in case of infection one way or the other.

Driving home by myself wasn't a great problem. The skies were leaden grey with rain so there was no hassle from the glaring light of earlier.

It was three in the afternoon when I returned to the sauna atmosphere of my home. Maisy Jane had her music blaring, singing along to Frankie Goes to Hollywood's *Relax*. When I say singing, it was more like some demented animal in pain.

I opened the door, intending to ask her to tone it down as I was ready for a nap.

'Sure, Kimmy. No hassles.'

At that moment, she realised something and tried vainly to hide a hair dryer . . . *my* hair dryer.

'What's that doing down here?' I demanded, shouting over the din.

'It's mine . . . just looks like yours.' It was a pathetic attempt to worm her way out of my accusation. Besides, hers had been on the stairs earlier and was nothing like my own.

'Oh. Even to having my initials on the handle?' The nail varnish letters glistened in the light.

There was no way for her to deny it now and she knew it. She turned the radio off. The silence was absolute.

I reached over to grab my property. I really didn't need this confrontation right now.

'How did you get this, Maisy Jane? My room was locked.'

She stood up defensively, but backed away, sensing my fury. I was taller than her and a darn sight fitter. When she almost tripped over a bag of hair rollers, any thought of arguing with me seemed to evaporate.

'My dryer is busted. I . . . I . . . used Joe's spare keys. I know where they're kept. Besides, you and that French girl have so much stuff, I figured you wouldn't mind if I loaned it.'

So MJ had been using Ludavine's possessions as well. Then there was my missing body wash and a few other items I assumed I'd misplaced.

'I've half a mind to arrest you, Maisy Jane. What were you thinking? Stealing from a police officer?'

'I was only loani . . . '

I held up my fist before speaking slowly and quietly; slowly because I wished to make certain Joe's girlfriend understood and quietly because I'd found it was often scarier that shouting.

'Never . . . ever . . . enter my room again.'

She gulped and nodded as I left. Once in my bedroom, I made a mental note to buy a padlock to supplement the integrated door lock, then flopped down on the bed, fully dressed.

★   ★   ★

I must have nodded off despite being so worked up. I never slept during the daytime.

A polite knock half-roused me. I felt terrible. Another knock. 'Kimberly. It's Ludavine.'

I opened my eyes. Things weren't right with my vision.

'Kimberly?'

My LED clock was fuzzy. Six twenty-five? Surely not.

'Coming,' I tried to say, loudly. Even that came out wrong. It was dark all around as I struggled to my feet.

'Wash ish it?' I asked, unlocking the door. The light from the landing bulb was blinding so I retreated into the shadows.

'It's Maisy Jane. I catch her to re-put my things back in my chambre . . . my bedroom. She tell me you have a fight with her. She is thief, non?'

Then she paused. 'Kimberly. What is wrong?' Her hand reached in to flip the light switch.

She stared at my face, put her hand to her mouth and gasped, 'Mon Dieu!'

'Ludavine. Wash you staring at?' My voice was all slurred as if I'd been drinking. I hadn't.

I spun round to the cheval mirror with my scarves draped over the corner.

'Hell!' I exclaimed. Another face looked at me — one that was grossly misshapen; just like the reflections in a fun house mirror.

The left eye was sagging, my mouth agape and also drooping. Even the left eyebrow was wrong.

Ludavine quickly apologised, putting her arm around me. 'I am thinking you 'ave ze accident vasculaire cérébral. Sorry. I cannot recall ze expression en anglais.'

Standing there in shock, there was only one word that sprang to mind. I wrote it on a notepad, before dropping the pen from my shaking hand.

'Bah oui, Kimberly. That is ze word. You 'ave a stroke.'

4

My knees felt like jelly. A stroke? My hand grabbed the door handle to steady myself. Strokes only happened to old people, didn't they?

Ludavine's face showed her concern for me.

'Will I call un medecin?'

A doctor? Yes. I had Doctor Little's card in my Filofax. Scrambling to find it in my bag, I removed the book and my mobile. Ludavine dialled, passing me the phone.

'Doctor Lidd . . . Isch Kimba . . . '
This wasn't working. My mouth felt as if it was full of chewy gum. All that was coming out was gibberish.

Consequently, I thrust the phone to Ludavine who luckily understood what needed doing.

'Bonsoir, Monsieur le Docteur. 'Allo. I am a friend of Kimberly Frost. She

95

has a problem with her face. It has fallen on ze left side; her eye, her mouth. Is zis a . . . ' she checked my scribbled word, 'a stroke?'

I heard his echoey reply. 'Can she move her arms and legs?'

I tried them. Hands too. All OK.

'Pas de problème . . . What is that? You speak with Kimberly?'

The phone was given back.

'Listen, Kimberly. Do not, I repeat, do not panic. It's not a stroke. I suspect there's a problem with your facial nerves. It isn't life-threatening. I understand you're scared and anxious, though there is nothing either of us can do to change it. Not tonight, anyway.'

Even with his reassuring words, I felt worried as anything.

'It's facial paralysis and chances are it's temporary. Come in tomorrow as we arranged. Can your friend stay with you?'

Ludavine could hear the question. She nodded.

'Yesh.'

'Good. Try to relax. Some wine, perhaps? I'll see you tomorrow. Don't be alarmed. We'll sort this out together.'

My eye was watering plus I suspected I was drooling a bit. Ludavine dabbed my chin with a tissue then forced a smile.

Trying to do the same didn't work. Her guarded response told me that. I understood then how it must have appeared; one side of my lips raised, the other unmoving. There was an image of some terrifying creature from those Hammer Horror films Dad used to watch.

I glanced at the mirror for a second. It was sickening. I burst into tears. Kimberly . . . the monster with half a face. Struggling to calm down, I wondered if ringing Dad was an option. No — he was busy with Mum and her illness. Maybe tomorrow when things were clearer about my condition.

Barry? Yes. He'd be here in a flash.

With faltering words, it was possible to make Ludavine understand. She opened the Filofax at B, then dialled him. She seemed puzzled before disconnecting.

'Is wrong number? A woman, she answers. Al . . . i . . . son?'

Barry's ex? Surely not.

We rang back. This time Barry answered and spoke to Ludavine. He agreed to come to me once my housemate had explained the situation.

In a way it was a relief, though the question remained; why was Alison there?

Maisy Jane was clomping around downstairs. There was no way I wanted her involved when Barry arrived. Like a true friend, Ludavine stepped forward to call down that I was unwell.

Maisy Jane retorted with the words, 'Good, but it better not be contagious,' prior to slamming the lounge room door and retreating back to her own boudoir. Frankie's *Relax* started to play for the dozenth time.

As for Ludavine, I was very impressed as well as grateful. We usually exchanged fewer than a dozen words. Like me, she kept to herself. In high school they'd taunted me with the name The Frost Queen due to me being a loner. I hadn't minded. It was way better than Frosty the Snowman which had followed me through my years at primary.

'Thank you,' I tried to say.

Ludavine remained with me until we heard the front door. She dashed downstairs. Maisy Jane opened the lounge door but was told the caller was for me, not her.

I heard Ludavine ask if he was Barry, in that beautiful, melodic voice of hers. 'Come up ze stairs, please.'

He seemed reluctant but followed her up.

He'd once berated me for my choice of shared accommodation. 'You should find yourself a bed-sit, like me. No need to share with strangers.' He was adamant that we had our own lives to live and all we needed was one another. Where did Alison fit in to that declaration?

Every footstep as he came closer now made me so frightened that I'd done the wrong thing by asking him to come.

What if . . . ? It was too late. He was on the landing.

'Barry?' I tried to articulate. My lovely boyfriend took one long look at my face before pushing Ludavine aside and leaving.

Half way down the stairs, he paused.

'Don't phone me again, Kimberly. You and I are finished.'

The shock hit me so hard, I couldn't breathe. Then the front door slammed. Just like that my 'lovely' boyfriend had dumped me like a bag of rubbish in a wheelie bin. How could he be so callous? The answer didn't matter.

He wasn't worth crying over, I told myself for as many seconds as I could. Then I felt my body convulse. Ludavine held me close.

'He is a nothing, Kimberly. He is ze arrogant pork.'

I had to laugh at that. Or at least try. I grabbed my pen and paper.

I think you meant to say 'arrogant pig'. But yes, he's an 'arrogant pork' too.

Ludavine read it and agreed. It broke the tension.

'You are better without 'im, Kimberly. Is zere anyone else I can call for you?'

I thought. There was Mark. He might be at Headquarters. So I dialled and Ludavine talked to him, again relating my dilemma.

He must have asked to have a word with me.

'Kimberly?' he asked in a gentle tone.

'Yesh.'

'I'm with your father at the hospital. We'll come straight round. Pack as much as you can. You're coming home with us. No arguments.'

I wasn't going to argue. Ludavine had already done more than I could possibly have expected. It wouldn't be fair to impose any longer.

'OK.' It was a relief. Mark had taken charge. It was precisely what I needed at this traumatic time.

By the time Dad and Mark arrived, I'd made a few decisions about my immediate future, as well as packing three suitcases with clothing and toiletries.

Whatever this mysterious affliction was, there was no possibility of me dealing with it alone in this place over the forthcoming days and nights.

My parents had told me many times that I was welcome to return to Bromyard so, pride swallowed, it was time to accept. It wasn't as though I was an invalid . . . simply a woman with a facial problem.

Ludavine let them in. With no sign of aversion, they embraced me. Mark seemed especially concerned, unlike that shockingly callous reaction from Barry; a man I had thought loved me.

Before we could all leave, Joe and Maisy Jane appeared on the landing. Joe was angry, although his manner altered slightly when he witnessed my not-so-stunning face under the single light bulb. Ludavine moved up by my side.

'What's going on, Kimberly? How dare you accuse my girlfriend of theft! And what's wrong with your face?'

'It's what the cow deserves,' Maisy Jane taunted, standing arm in arm with Joe.

'Shut up, MJ,' said Joe.

Ludavine spoke up for me as Dad and Mark were totally in the dark. 'Kimberly is moving, Joe. Your girl-friend . . . she takes the things from our rooms. She is bad person. And I go to move aussi. This is bad place.'

I squeezed Ludavine's hand, grateful for her support.

That shocked him, probably more so than the sight of the two silent men who he'd never met. He was clearly outnumbered.

Undeterred, he played his trump card.

'You can't leave — either of you. There's a lease.'

I refused to humiliate myself with

slurred speech in front of anyone that didn't have my best interests at heart. Passing Joe a note I'd already written, I stepped back into the half shadow.

He read it aloud. '*Our agreements expired two months ago. Looks like you and your useless girlfriend will have the house completely to yourselves now, Joe.*'

MJ was incensed.

'I'm not useless. Tell her, Joe.'

He responded before I could.

'Actually, you are, MJ. Sitting around here all day like the Queen of Sheba. You'll have to get yourself a job. I can't afford this place alone.'

Maisy Jane's eyes opened wide. Her smug expression had gone.

Any strength I had for further fights had gone too. It was time to leave. Dad picked up a suitcase and, arm firmly around me, led me past Joe and MJ. Mark and Ludavine followed with the rest of my personal possessions in their hands.

My father, who'd not uttered a word

until now, stopped at the top of the stairs.

He spoke in a subdued voice; a monotone with veiled strength that showed he wasn't messing around.

'I'll be back tomorrow to move my daughter's furniture out — and yours too, young lady, if you like.' He indicated Ludavine. 'As for you, mate, if you don't want any trouble, you'll make certain that thieving magpie of a girlfriend doesn't put her purple claws on anything of my daughter's. Anything. Do you understand?'

Joe nodded meekly.

I saw my father in a totally new way. I hadn't invented the quiet, threatening manner I thought of as my strength. He had. I'd simply copied it.

Once outside, Ludavine confessed to my father.

'Monsieur Frost. I do not 'ave somewhere to go. I cannot leave still.'

'Just get into the car for a moment, Miss. Where it's warm. I'm going to use Kimberly's phone to ring a friend of mine, I am. She lives nearby and I happen to know she's searching for a young lady to rent a room in her house.

'Mark? Could you get the bags — and you, Kimberly, can show me how to use this gadget.' It was obvious Dad hadn't used a mobile before.

Within moments we were all in Mark's car where my father explained that there was a place for Ludavine to rent if she wanted. She was overjoyed — more so when Dad advised her that it was larger and tidier. 'Adele is happy to charge the same rent as you and Kimberly paid.'

Ludavine was very pleased.

'Zis Adele. You know her well, Monsieur Frost?'

'She's my secretary at work. Lovely lady. A widow. What's more I think you will have lots to talk about, Miss Ludavine.'

Ludavine was puzzled. 'Pourquoi, Monsieur? I 'ave problem speaking ze English.'

'Adele is from Brittany. She's French.'

Hearing that, Ludavine leaned over to the front seat to give my father a kiss on each cheek. She clapped her little hands with joy.

'Is that OK then, Miss Ludavine?'

'Bah, certainement. I am . . . how do you say? Over ze moon.'

Dad and Ludavine chatted for a while longer before Dad wrote down Adele's phone number and address. The rest was up to her. I walked her back to my former home where we said goodbye.

'Is not 'goodbye', Kimberly. Is au revoir, until we meet again.'

Returning to Mark's car I snuggled into the back seat to wave to her. Mark turned the ignition on. He was very quiet but I wasn't feeling much like a chat either.

It was strange how this evening had revealed unexpected details about the people in my life, shattering some perceptions yet forging new ones at the same time.

* * *

My namesake was beginning to crystal-
lise on the car windows because it was a
clear, moonlit night. Despite my jumper
and camel coat, I shivered. I cast one
last look at my home since 1993, with
Ludavine still waving in the distance.

Dad had moved to be next to me on
the back seat. He explained Mark had
dropped him at the hospital before
spending the day at police HQ.

'Wash latesht wi girls?' I asked Mark
in an attempt to be normal.

He appeared to understand my
gibberish much better than I expected.
At the same time, I understood that
Dad had his own struggles with my
condition. He was holding my hand so
tightly at times, I had to nudge him.

'The latest with Scarlett and Crystal?' Mark repeated for my father's
benefit. 'We tracked the computer
address that was used in Ludlow. It was
a dead end, just like the two phones at
the Sandersons. Very frustrating. And

still no proper ransom demand, only that fake one. It's a puzzle and the longer things go on ... well, you understand.'

It was almost three days since the abduction.

'At least Mr Bowen is back home,' he added as we drove through the darkened countryside. Skeletal walls seemed to hem us in as Mark drove along the familiar road. There was little traffic coming our way so he was able to keep the high beam on for the majority of our journey. I felt safe with him.

Thinking about it, I always had.

In an attempt to not dwell on my condition, I revisited the facts the police had gathered. It allowed me to feel of some use. All the time there was that worry of what the children were going through, snatched from the people and places. they knew. They must be so terrified. My own problems paled when I considered theirs.

I prayed Dr Little would sort me out

quickly so I could return to help. Doing my job was impossible like this. Two or three days. Hopefully, things would be right by then. Hopefully.

Despite sleeping this afternoon, I must have dozed off once more. Dad nudged me.

'We're home, kitten. Bromyard.'

Even though The Falcon and Queen's Arms would be busy, the rest of my home town would be quiet, especially on this chilly evening. Front gardens and windows with twinkling lights didn't help my mood. This was Christmas time for everyone except the Bowens. It was so wrong. As for the horrifying thought that those girls had been harmed . . .

Dad and Mark carried my things inside, then Dad went out to the kitchen to start on dinner. I suspected it wouldn't be up to mum's cordon bleu best, but I wasn't concerned in the least. It was good to be here.

When I took my jacket off, Mark made no move to do the same. Asking him why, he replied in a concerned tone.

'I'm going back into HQ, Kimberly. Your dad'll drive you to the doctor's tomorrow. He's going to look after you, kid.'

He helped with my baggage and was polite enough, yet there was something he was keeping hidden from me. I could sense it.

Then he added, 'When I see your Detective Sergeant, I'll bring him up to date and that you'll be at Dr Little's tomorrow if he wants to catch up with you. Your dad's not an ogre, Kimberly. He cares for you deeply.'

'Never shaid he wash an ogre.' My attempt at smiling failed miserably. 'I'm ogre now.'

Mark encompassed me in his arms.

'You'll always be beautiful to me, Kimberly.' He kissed me on the left cheek. I couldn't feel it, though. I turned. His face was so close.

'Mark . . . ' I began just as his lips brushed against mine. That's all they did — touch; yet it was enough to give my fragile psyche a real boost.

'See you tomorrow, kid.'

And he was gone, leaving me totally confused. What had just happened?

Dad's voice roused me from my daydream.

'Kimberly. Could you come here? This damn kettle. I can never get the thing to work.'

I laughed to myself. Even that noise came out wrong. Dad was not a kitchen person, but give him the task of designing an injector system for a helicopter and he'd be in his element. I guessed that me being here would be good for both of us.

As I went to him, I wondered. Was Mark simply being supportive after me being struck down with this affliction — or was he, as Mum said, in love with me?

5

The following day, Dad and I set off early for Hereford. It was a spectacular sunrise. To be with Dad again in his old Mazda 626 felt very comforting.

He explained that he'd been down to the works while I was getting ready. It was about a mile away. My keys had been given to two men to go to Cygnet Place and collect my furniture, such as it was, as well as anything else of mine. Ludavine would be there to keep an eye on the devious Maisy Jane and point out what belonged to me.

I wasn't bothered about salvaging anything in the fridge. MJ had probably demolished anything edible and even if it was still there, I didn't fancy the half-eaten chocolate any longer.

When I protested about men going through my personal things, he shushed me.

'Adele is going too. I thought she could chat to Ludavine and, if your friend wants, they could drop her possessions at Adele's place on the way back. It made sense to kill two birds at the same time, it did.'

★   ★   ★

Dr Little was awaiting me in the surgery, ushering us in before too many curious people wondered why I was wearing a scarf around my face. Technically, he wasn't scheduled for his clinic until eleven so he'd made special arrangements for me. For that, I was grateful.

Dad was by my side as I unwrapped my face.

Dr Little was thorough and professional, with questions galore that I struggled to answer — or write down when it became too difficult or exasperating. The drooling was a problem, as had been eating, last night and at breakfast. My sense of taste was haywire too.

Then came the physical examination.

'Kimberly,' he said as he sat back in his swivel chair and interlocked his fingers in front of him. 'What I suspected last night seems to be the case. You have a facial paralysis called Bell's Palsy. Have you heard of it?'

I glanced at Dad. We shook our heads.

The doctor went to a battered filing cabinet by the curtained window of his consulting room. It was only then that I noticed his slight limp. He must have been in his early sixties.

'Here are some booklets which will explain the condition in more detail. It's not that uncommon.'

Dad jumped in with his queries before I could.

'How long will this last, Doctor? How can you cure it?'

'Depends. We've caught it early, plus your daughter is young and fit. Her chances of a full recovery are good. I'll prescribe corticosteroids to reduce the nerve inflammation just here.' He tapped his temple. 'The seventh cranial nerve splits into branches that control muscles for frowning, moving your eyelid, tear production and your lips. Also, as you said, your sense of taste.'

My dad showed his anxiousness for my well-being in his almost frantic desire to do something. It might have been heightened due to his inability to help Mum as much as he thought he should.

'Can't she have antibiotics to cure it? My wife is in hospital with bronchitis — ' he began.

Dr Little held up his hand. 'From what Kimberly told me yesterday, she had a cold a few weeks ago. The cause of this problem is most likely a virus. Rest assured, Mr Frost, I'll do a blood test, although the body generally fixes itself. As I said a few weeks. Almost certainly, in two months.'

Weeks? Months? I said a naughty word, though even that came out wrong. If no one understands you, is it proper swearing?

'Kimberly!' Dad admonished me. 'There's no need for that sort of language, especially here.' I guess some things weren't that difficult to say after all. I apologised, before writing my own question down. *What can I do about my eye?*

Dr Little examined it more closely this time.

'I'll give you some drops to help with lubrication. Then some tape to hold the eyelid closed when you're asleep.'

'Is there nothing more you can do, Doctor? She's a policewoman.'

'I am aware of that, Mr Frost.' He stroked his stubble-covered chin. 'There might be something. The physio department at the hospital have some exercises you can do that might help you regain your speech faster. I'll make a referral.'

We thanked him and I wrapped myself up again. It was time to visit Mum. Not that I wished to see her as I was — yet it made sense, if we were going to the County Hospital anyway.

Also, it had a pharmacy for the steroids and such.

It was while I was getting into Dad's car that the scarf was caught in the wind and slipped. A mother and her son were passing. The young boy saw my face then drew back in shock, bursting into tears.

'Cover yourself up,' the mother told me sharply. 'You scared my Tommy.'

Dad was about to reply in kind but I put my hand on his arm to restrain him.

He faced me, saying loudly enough for her to hear, 'You're right, Kimberly. She's not worth it.'

In the car, he rubbed his wrist and grinned.

'Damn it, kitten. That's one strong grip you've got there. You really do. Glad I'm not some villain you're dealing with. I may not have told you recently that I'm so proud of you, and I'm truly sorry. I should be saying that every single day. I'll try to be a better father in the future.'

On the short drive, I had a chance to reflect on the doctor's prognosis. There was a damp, drizzly fog shrouding the sombre streets. I hated the winter. It drained the life from me. To my mind, Christmas lights and decorations only highlighted the dreariness of everything else — the never-ending nights and bleak, chilling winds.

Today was especially bad. It only reminded me of my own gloomy state.

Forget finding the missing girls. What could I possibly do like this? Interrogation was out of the question. Even the sight of me would have some low-life screaming about police brutality. When it came to police, there were the good, the bad — and now the ugly. Me.

At the hospital, Dad went off to break the news to Mum about her not-so-beautiful little girl. He'd been told this morning that she was much improved and was expected to be discharged on Tuesday.

The doctor had told us he'd fax the sick note to my HQ; two weeks for starters. He was also letting my DS in on the latest regarding my state of health. I wondered what Steven would make of it all. We were already down a few officers from the usual winter ailments. That I was now off ill would be the icing on the cake.

The physio receptionist was very kind, booking me in for an assessment with my initial session scheduled for late Wednesday morning. That I'd have an hour round trip from Bromyard each time, wasn't a problem. Although I was off sick, I didn't feel unwell. It was simply my damn face.

Mark rang on my mobile to get an update on my doctor visit. I couldn't really answer apart from a few garbled words. It was definitely a communication breakdown. Time to see Mum.

I'd found a notepad that morning buried underneath blankets in the bedding box of my childhood bedroom. Mothers keep all sorts; old toys and dolls, school books with gold stars. On the front cover, I'd printed *This book belongs to the ravishing, marvellous Kimberly Frost — 1985*. There was a cut-out drawing of The Frost Queen glued on too. I'd decorated it back in school, still full of teenage enthusiasm.

On impulse, I'd brought it with me today to help with communication. The cover was meant to remind me of who I remained inside. Sometimes it did help; that was, until I caught sight of my reflection. My new life was going to take some getting used to.

We closed the curtains around Mum's bed for the big reveal. Her expression, suppressed though it was, said it all; pity, surprise, anger.

She reached up from her bed to dab the corner of my mouth. It was demeaning but loving at the same time. Mum began to ask questions, Dad answered, then we all sat down and read through the literature Dr Little had given us. It made me even more depressed.

'It says here,' Mum commented, 'that it might start with a pain behind the ear. Did you have that, Kimberly?'

I nodded. At the time, I'd thought it was from my cold or something minor. Also, I now realised my hearing had changed, making me sensitive to some sounds. Yet it was my inability to smile that upset me the most.

When a nurse pulled aside the blue curtain, I tried to avert my face. I was too slow.

'Bell's Palsy?' she asked, concern in her voice. 'It'll get better, love. We see all sorts in here. You're that police-woman in the papers. I recognise you.'

I began to panic.

'Sorry. You haven't heard?' she explained. 'Morning paper. Those horrid kidnappers mentioned you again. Sent a school photo from Queen Elizabeth High. Why are they picking on you?'

It was a good question. One I could only guess the answer to.

Dad spoke up. 'We believe that it's a

distraction. The criminal is playing mind games with my daughter because she's the only one to have made any breakthrough so far.' He paused. 'Maybe I've said too much.'

The nurse returned with the newspaper. Admittedly it wasn't page one, and the photo was flattering. It was a good thing they didn't print one of me as I looked right now.

''eeling shick . . . ' I covered my mouth. The nurse grabbed a bowl just in time.

After being cleaned up like some baby, Mum told Dad to take me home.

'I'll be fine here, Ted. You go and look after Kimberly.' Her coughing had stopped, although her breathing was still laboured from time to time. Unlike me, she appeared much better.

Dad reluctantly agreed. 'Come on, kitten. We'll stop at the pharmacy first. The we'll get you settled in back home. All your stuff from that house should be there by now. It'll be just like old times. Maybe a game of Monopoly and catch up on the latest gossip from the old town?'

I tried to smile again. Dad hated playing my favourite game. He was making a real effort.

Provided you do the talking, I wrote in my notebook.

Dad took my hand.

'Makes a change from school days. You never shut up then. You and Mark.'

Yeah, I thought. Me and Mark were inseparable back then.

I wished I could read his mind right now. What would he be thinking about me?

* * *

The rest of Monday was uneventful, thank goodness. My possessions from Cygnet Place arrived and were stacked in the hall, squeezed into my bedroom or stored in one side of our double garage. It took Dad and me an hour or so to re-create my happy place. I covered up the mirror in my bedroom.

There was no point using it, I'd decided.

After that, I made a late lunch. In a way, I was pleased to be in the cosy warmth rather than traipsing around outside doing police work. It made me guilty. More so when DS Cameron arrived to see how I was.

I tried to be positive as we all sat down to Christmas cake and a drink. Then a mouthful of coffee spilt from my lips onto the floor.

I wiped my mouth then the carpet, not daring to even glance at him in pure shame.

'Can I suggest something, Kimberly? It might be presuming too much. We've only been together a few days so please don't think I'm insulting you in any way. Have you considered a training mug for toddlers? It has a lid and a small opening. Or you could even use a straw?'

Sitting down again, I wrote down, Yeah. *Training mug. It makes sense.* Drinking tea or coffee through a straw seemed even stranger to me.

'I have one at home. Well, not me personally. My daughter's ten. She doesn't use it now. And it's clean. Mauve, just like your blouse.'

I wrote, *Blouse is cerise*.

He grinned. 'Sorry. Cerise, then. My missus always wants things to match. Colour coordination, she calls it. Especially curtains and cushions and . . . I'm rabbiting on, aren't I?'

'Jusha liddle.' I drew a smiley face on my notepad.

'Consider it done, Kimberly. I'll drop it off tomorrow. Been running all over the county with sightings of the girls. I swear this Lollipop Man is making them up, making us run in circles.'

'Sthill no ranshom?'

'No. And between you and me, that's bad. Not that the Bowens are millionaires, but he does have a good job and Candice's family are well to do. She inherited quite a bit when her gran passed away. That friend of hers, Rhonda? She's there a lot of the time.'

I crossed my fingers to show him that I was hoping for the best too.

Dad was listening but could offer no suggestions. Unless there were developments, we all realised the trail was getting far too cold.

Mark didn't come round that night although he did speak to Dad. It would have been good to see him, but he was busy. Besides, he might be having second thoughts after his unexpected confessions of the past few days.

Speech exercises plus massages in front of my uncovered bedroom mirror showed me the true extent of my affliction.

I set the tape recorder up and said aloud, 'Day two.' The leaflets suggested speaking slowly. My idea was that I could use recordings to judge improvement, or lack thereof.

The letters p, b, w, r and f were hard to enunciate because of my flaccid lips. It was ironic that I couldn't pronounce the name of my condition properly.

Worse was the eye problem. Exasperated at splashing the drops everywhere, I accepted Dad's kind offer to put them in. Drinking was infuriating, too. *Roll on training mug*, I thought angrily.

On impulse, I took the top off my favourite lipstick before deciding against it. Who'd be interested now? My life was stuffed — well and truly.

As for that kiss from Mark . . . well, that's all it was. Best of intentions, but that was Mark — a friend for all seasons.

★   ★   ★

During the night, we had our first decent snowfall; a couple of inches remained until lunchtime when the warming December sun melted most of it, leaving greying slush in the shadows.

Staying home while Dad took time off work again to collect Mum was a bit of a cop-out, I knew. Truth was, I felt very unsociable. Even knowing it would be temporary didn't help my state of mind. Rationalising that it wasn't as devastating as cancer or some terminal illness wasn't much use to my selfish attitude. People would be uncomfortable around me, possibly ignoring me because I couldn't express myself normally.

Then I remembered the terror I had felt when Ludavine thought it was a stroke. This was bad enough. How could I possibly cope with something as life-changing as that? I thought of Ludavine and Mrs Wu. They spoke in a 'funny way' and I hadn't always accepted that. Geordie accents, Australian accents . . . they were all different.

I made some lunch, ready to welcome my parents. By the time they'd arrived, I was marginally better. Dad must have understood how down I was.

'I found something in the attic when I was searching for decorations. Thought it might cheer you up. Some stuff from when you were younger.'

I opened the cardboard box. My eyes lit up. It had all my *Wonder Woman* videos and toy dolls in it, as well as some comics.

While I was growing up, the super-heroine's comics sort of inspired me and improved my reading. I used to say I had an invisible plane, and had pretended to be looking for it when Mum caught me nosing around in cupboards for presents before Christmas and my birthday.

I had my collection of her Amazonian artefacts too; the magic golden 'lasso of truth' which was a yellow clothes line, a tiara I'd made of cardboard and elastic and my 'indestructible amazonium' bracelets which Dad had fabricated at the factory for me.

The strangest thing was that her creator, Charles Moulton, was the pen-name for a man who helped invent the lie detector. It was a real-life version of her golden lariat which compelled baddies to tell the truth.

Maybe she inspired me to become a crime fighter. I wasn't sure. In any case I wasn't ever going to be running around in a skimpy costume — especially not in this weather.

I could do with being her once again, I wrote. The tiara fitted, but the bracelets were too small.

'Shame,' I said, touched by some nostalgia. Dad nodded.

We ate before Dad returned to work, worried that without his guiding hand, the factory might have ground to a halt.

It was great to see my mother back to her usual bubbly, chatty self. I'd chosen to have a sloppy day; comfiest jeans and furry bunny slippers. I was watching some inane game show with Mum and our cat when the doorbell rang.

Mum answered it. She invited our visitors in. There were two of them, from their voices. I sat up before Mum ushered them in.

'DC Frost. Good to see you.' Detective Chief Inspector Aldershot shook my hand before taking the seat my mother indicated. My DS sat by his side. If the chief were concerned about my facial paralysis, he didn't show it. It was a fair assumption that Steven had warned him.

'I was sorry to hear of your illness, Kimberly. And yours too, Mrs Frost. If there was any way I could avoid intruding at this time, I would, especially since you are officially on leave.'

'Whash the . . . ' I realised 'problem' would be unintelligible to say so I wrote it down.

'Kimberly. We need your help.'

'Not much help like thish,' I struggled to say. I sensed rather than felt spittle running down the left side of my chin, wiping it as covertly as I could.

'Kimberly. My father had a stroke last year which affected him in a similar way to you. I don't want to put you through this, believe me — there's been a ransom demand at last, but this . . . ' He glanced at my mother, conscious that he shouldn't use the swear word he wanted to. 'This Lollipop Man has insisted that you deliver the money. You and you alone. The Bowens want to pay

132

up, against my official advice. In this case I confess I'm inclined to agree — off the record of course. Somehow, and we don't understand how, he's aware you're on a leave of absence.'

My mum spoke up quickly. 'How is that even possible? A leak in the police force itself?'

Her tone was more defensive than angry. I felt the same. My life was somehow on full display to this insidious criminal. Was he watching Mark and me the other night from his car? Was he spying on me right now?

I wandered over to the window to survey the street. No strange cars apart from the DCI's.

'Rest assured, Mrs Frost. Within the police, only the two of us were aware of Kimberly's absence yesterday evening. That's when when the demand was delivered. Dr Little's fax came straight through to me. Since then I've told others that you are on sick leave but that's it. Nothing about the facial paralysis.'

133

The Chief Inspector was clearly very concerned. The thought that there was some mole or informant within the force was unthinkable to me and, I was certain, to him too.

'Then how?' I asked.

'We're trying to ascertain that. In the meantime, the Bowens have been given until Thursday to raise fifty thousand pounds. This Lollipop person will give us directions for you to deliver the cash, then the girls will be freed . . . we pray.'

Mum stared at me. 'Kimberly. It's too dangerous. You're hardly in a position to defend yourself if things go wrong.'

I made my mind up. The girls needed me.

'OK, I'll do it.'

My DS thanked me.

'Good to hear, DC Frost. There is one more thing. Unfortunately you might not be very pleased when we tell you.'

I took a sip of water through a straw. Some sixth sense told me he would probably be right.

6

Wednesday saw me driving to the County Hospital for my first session. I'd decided to go alone. For the past few days I'd been relying on others far too much.

Delivering the ransom money should be straightforward. That wasn't my concern. If things became awkward, I could still run and I could fight as well as most men.

When I arrived at the physiotherapy department, there was a warm greeting from all the staff. At least they could understand what I was going through and not talk down to me.

At the same time, I noticed a familiar face in a corner chatting to a white-garbed woman, probably some doctor. I recognised him from somewhere. He had a blond, Nordic appearance, hair combed and cut immaculately. His suit was smart too, with an open-necked white shirt and scarf casually wound around his neck.

Two of the nurses did a detailed assessment of what I could and couldn't do at present. They called it the baseline. They took Polaroids of me smiling and frowning. I showed them the training mug Steven had brought me. They didn't laugh. I'd learned a lot from the leaflets, though they added some practical suggestions for eating and drinking.

After a while, I was led over to a seat by a box-type machine. Other patients were lifting weights or on treadmills or step-machines. There was a hydro pool in an adjoining annexe.

'Did you bring something to read, Kimberly? Like we suggested.'

I had, although I wasn't sure why. Police files from my attaché case didn't sound like a relaxing choice, yet it made sense. When I suggested that I could still be useful by double checking information from the abduction investigation, the DCI had reluctantly agreed, on the condition that it remained confidential. Not even Mark was to know. It made sense to have a collator.

I can be your secret weapon, I wrote on my notepad before showing it to him.

'Makes sense. He probably thinks you're off the case and is taking control by making you bring the money. If you can work undercover, then that might be to our advantage.'

The nurses moved the huge machine so it was by my side. There was a cone they put by my head, just around where the nerve split near my ear. Switching it on, there was a low hum. That was it; no sparks or heat. I'd been told it was a magnetometer; a gadget that set up a magnetic field that was somehow supposed to stimulate the nerve to work again.

I recalled some boring Physics class where we moved a magnet through a coil of wire to make an electric current. Since we had electricity in our nerves, a magnetic field kind of made sense.

The most important thing was that it might help. Quite frankly if a magic unicorn had appeared, offering to sort my face out, I would have kissed his nose and told him to go for it.

Half an hour, three days a week; it looked as if this was going to be my routine for a while — with the occasional delivery of money to an abductor in case I became bored.

Whatever it takes, I decided, beginning to pore over the dozen or so pages from the files that I'd brought with me. Somewhere there just might be some clue that hadn't yet been picked up on.

I began reading, then examining photos. There were shoe prints inside and outside the Bowen home, the empty bedroom and laundry window.

An inconsistency with one picture piqued my interest. I made a mental note to investigate it further. There were size six trainer prints alongside and on top of those of the intruders.

Another person, standing watch? Possibly a woman or youth? I couldn't imagine Mrs Bowen wearing them, and the fact that they over-printed the other prints suggested the owner was there at the same time. Jessica had left the week before. Besides, she was a size four.

Then there was the personal question. Why was I being persecuted by this Lollipop Man and how was he so familiar with my situation?

★ ★ ★

The thirty-odd minutes flew by as I was so engrossed in the files. Did I feel any different? The answer was no. It wasn't a miracle cure. Mum had reminded me last night of my tendency to be impatient.

'Do you remember how upset you were after your first day at school, Kimberly?'

I'd forgotten. Well, I was pretty young at the time.

'You threw one of your infamous

tantrums once you came home, stamping and pouting. Being the bossy madam you were, you blamed me. 'Mummy,' you said. 'You told me that when I went to school, I could write and read: But I can't. You fibbed.' Of course, I tried to explain that it would take longer than one day to which you, my darling Kimberly, had to have the last word.'

Go on, Mum. It's not as though I have the last word any more, I wrote.

'Let's see. 'Well, it shouldn't,' were your exact words. 'I need to read and write *now*. I got 'portant stuff to do.''

It sounded far-fetched though I did recall being a right little pain as a girl. Mum used to joke about Helen of Troy telling me that if she had the face that launched a thousand ships, my pout would sink all of them without a trace. Thinking about my face at the moment, I guessed things hadn't changed much.

★ ★ ★

Thursday arrived. Almost a week since Scarlett and Crystal disappeared. It was the day of the ransom delivery and I wasn't feeling anywhere near as positive as I had been.

Mark collected me early in his car. Mine was twice as comfortable, yet he refused to be seen in a car with a pink leather steering wheel. The front passenger seat had been hastily cleared of computer junk like mother boards, father boards and, for all I knew, baby boards too. They were now scattered across the back seat.

He tipped some water from an old Pepsi bottle over the windscreen in an attempt to remove the half-ton of salt and muck that taken up residence there.

When are you getting the washers fixed? I wrote, before making sure my gloves were snug.

He shrugged. 'The car heater's packed in too.'

I half grimaced. *Doesn't your girl-friend complain?* were my next written words.

He was de-misting the windows with a soggy sponge and tissues, and didn't notice my message at first. Once he did, he shifted into neutral before putting the key in the ignition.

'Girlfriend? Dunno. Why don't you ask her?'

This cryptic answer was way too irritating for me. This Frost Queen had never been an early morning girl.

Mark lowered the passenger side visor so that the mirror reflected my face. His insensitivity was totally out of order. Then I realised.

'You mean me?' I tried to say before dabbing my mouth where I could see saliva.

Instead of starting off, Mark took my hand in both of his.

'I've always loved you, Kimberly. Yeah, me, the ultimate geek with his ugly glasses. Maybe I should have confessed to you years ago but I was afraid. Better to have you as a friend than lose you completely. Let's face it, you tend to go through boyfriends like a box of Smarties.'

I blanched with anger, even though it was possibly true. I'd been too cool and distant for my more passionate suitors. Was Mark right?

Shifting uncomfortably on the cold vinyl seat, I wondered if Mum were watching from the lounge window, puzzled by our non-departure.

Instead of reacting verbally, I took a long look at my life. As in the situation with Barry, I was generally the 'dumpee' rather than the dumper. Terms like my schoolgirl nicknames of Ice-cool Frosty and Frigid Frosty had been thrown my way by a few so-called boyfriends, often because I preferred not to be as physical as they might have wanted. Those men had then moved on to more accommodating partners.

Mark had chosen not to be one of those fleeting romances. In many ways, he understood me better than I did myself. It had been his shoulder I'd cried on, far too many times. Nonetheless what sort of man, feeling the way he obviously did, would sit by quietly as I effused about the latest boy or man in my life?

I scribbled, *You certainly pick your moments*, then smiled weakly. Me at my most vulnerable, both physically and mentally, en route to deliver a crucial ransom with two girls' futures in the balance. Yeah. He really had.

'Now or never, Kimberly. Barry was the final straw. You have an uncanny knack of picking losers. You deserve much better — a man who understands and cares for you.'

'And atsh you?'

This was too much for me to process at this moment. I was furious at him for telling me this on today of all days, but a part of me understood his exasperation and why he'd done it. Regrettably, I couldn't walk away to think about our future.

Can we go now? I wrote. *Just take me to HQ. Do not say another word.*

7

The silence for that half hour was deafening. I sat, hunched up against the rigid passenger seat, partly from the cold, mainly from the overwhelming miasma in my head from too much information to deal with.

I let my mind go numb and focused instead on the blur of countryside rushing by the freezing window.

One comfort was that my damaged left side was against the window. At least the normal side was all Mark could see when he glanced over.

My thoughts wandered back to when we met in the first year at secondary school. I'd felt very alone, keen to find a friend. Mark had appeared to be alone too, being the tallest boy in our class and wearing specs just as I had back then.

'Hi,' I'd said, trying to engage him.

'I'm Kimberly. Some of the others said you're Greek. That's where the Olympics started, isn't it?'

He'd stared at me as if I was a rainbow-coloured polar bear before bending over to address me in a voice that was starting to break.

'I'm not Greek, you daft girl. I'm English, just like my parents,' was his dismissive retort.

'Then why did Billy Smith say . . . ?'

'He probably called me a geek. Do you know what a geek is? Like a wally, or a nerd. I study computers and radios and stuff. No one wants to be friends with a geek. Except possibly another geek.'

I'd thought about it before replying, 'Then I 'spose I'm another geek.' Hesitantly, I'd reached out to shake his hand. It was warm, just like his smile.

Reaching into my brand-new school bag, I'd removed my diary to write in it, sharing it with him. *Dear Diary. I made a new friend today. He's very tall and his name is* . . . 'What's your name?' I asked aloud.

'Mark. You do realise you're a very strange girl, Kimberly. Pretty, but very strange.'

★ ★ ★

At police headquarters we went our separate ways. Nothing further had been said. I must have appeared like some film star avoiding fans by wearing dark glasses and a head scarf, but it was better than wearing nothing over my features. People's opinions were less important to me than they had been when this affliction first struck.

How I'd get back to Bromyard was a problem to face later. Going home with Mark wasn't an option. Switching to thoughts of what I was going to do in the following hours suddenly made me shiver. After all, there was a chance that things might go awry.

My DCI and DS Cameron were waiting in the chief's office. Blinds were drawn. In an attempt to restrict operational integrity, they were the only officers who were aware of details.

'Kimberly. Good of you to join us. Are you still up for this?'

Removing my film star disguise, I nodded.

'Great. The rendezvous is scheduled for one o'clock. Saying that, LM might change time or place to wrong-foot us. He also might give you the runaround to make certain police aren't nearby to grab him once the exchange is made.

'W . . . whir . . . we here is it?' I managed to ask.

DS Cameron passed me a red manila folder.

'Here's his ransom request. Typewritten, with no useful prints. Plus there's a Polaroid of the girls holding yesterday's Herald.'

The note was precise and detached. It had been delivered downstairs by a courier who'd been paid in cash. He hadn't seen who'd done it. Talk about brazen.

Kimberly Frost must deliver fifty thousand pounds in used, unmarked, non-consecutive twenty-pound notes in an attaché bag at the following time and place. She must be alone and unarmed. No other police within two miles. Failure to comply and the girls will die.

Once I am satisfied there are no tricks, I will leave — unharmed and alone — or the girls will die.

Only my accomplice will be aware of the girls' location and will release them two hours after the payment is made if I give them a code to do so. Any interference and . . . well, you get the picture.

Not surprisingly, it was unsigned.

I studied the photo minutely. The children appeared to be healthy yet their eyes showed their fear. Their clothing appeared clean. They'd clearly been changed as there was no sign of the night clothes they'd been wearing.

Taking a pen from my bag, I asked, *Tell me we have a back-up plan. We can't let him walk away with the money without tracking him.*

I gave my book to the two officers to read.

'Your Mark has it in hand,' DCI Aldershot replied, pressing a buzzer which sounded in the next room. The connecting door was pushed open. My eyes met Mark's momentarily before I stared at the photo once more.

He placed a tiny chunk of metal on the desk. I guessed it was a miniature transmitter — a bug. It was less than a quarter of an inch in size and almost flat, with a thin wire . . . an aerial?

'Meet Tiny Tim.' He held it up. 'The money case looks normal enough, but I've hidden a transmitter like this within the lining. Range of five miles, and the battery will last at least four days, sending out a beep every ten seconds.'

The DCI clapped his massive hand on Mark's shoulder, almost knocking his glasses off.

'That's inspired. Splendid job, Mr Rathaway. Our villain walks off with the cash, not suspecting we're tracing his movements. Once the girls are released, we'll know exactly where he is, send in the SFOs to capture him while returning the lassies to their parents.'

That startled me. I didn't even know we had a team of Specialist Firearms Officers in Hereford. Then again, it made sense to bring in the big guns, so to speak. It was a high-profile crime and we couldn't afford to underestimate LM.

My DS asked the question on my numb lips.

'So what happens if the Bowen kids aren't released?'

'We arrest him. His strength has been his anonymity, with no one knowing who he really is. Once exposed he'll either tell us what we need or the great British public will. People will recognise him, mark my words. We'll unpick every facet of his life, where's he's been, who his friends are. We'll find them, DS Cameron. That's a promise.'

Steven had made the same promise

to Mrs Bowen almost a week ago. We were no closer, despite his reckless statement. Was the DCI's promise any more likely to be kept?

Mark opened a plastic bag he'd brought in with the leather case. Reaching in, he extracted a small microphone attached to a battery pack. There were straps as well.

I shuddered. When my superiors had visited me on Tuesday, they'd kept the worst till last. Not only was I dropping off the money, I was now being given a wire. If LM found that . . . well, let's say it wouldn't be good for my health.

'This will allow us to listen to everything that goes on. I'll fit it, if we could have some privacy. It needs to be well hidden under her clothes. Then I'll test the microphone.'

I wrote in my book and passed it over.

Steven read it aloud. 'Kimberly requests a woman police officer to attach it, Mark.'

My friend laughed. 'You're kidding, right? I've seen you in a bikini lots of times. It's not as though I'll be looking at any more than that.'

I pointed to my note and folded my arms.

This time it was the DCI's turn.

'Seems like she's insistent, young man. Friends or not, you're not touching her. I'll find a WPC who knows the procedure, Kimberly.'

Mark seemed upset. I saw it in his eyes. Normally, it wouldn't be a problem. He'd put suntan cream on me when our two families went on holiday. But today was different. It wouldn't feel proper for him to touch me, knowing the way he felt about me. Not dirty or anything; just wrong.

The three guys left, with me wondering if the future that Mark had feared might actually come true. Could he and I ever be in friends again?

★ ★ ★

On the way to the arranged rendezvous, we called to collect the money from the Bowens.

On opening the door, Candice Bowen put her arms around me. She led us through to the girls' bedroom where her husband was sitting on Scarlett's bed. Daniel Bowen was pale and very subdued, but stood politely to greet us all. He wasn't how I'd imagined him; black hair, greying at the temples as well as being considerably older than Candice. Love was unpredictable.

'It felt right to discuss what happens here, in their special place,' he explained, gazing around the room. Leaning across the bed, he picked up the talking bear, Teddy Ruxpin.

'Hello,' said the large toy, its mouth moving in time with the voice. 'Shall I tell you a story?' Daniel switched the bear off, dabbing his already red eyes. Then he composed himself and stood up to shake our hands. It was crowded in here despite the spaciousness of the room.

'DC Frost. Candice and I are extremely sorry that you have to be involved. Clearly you have your own problems now and have already done a lot to track the abductors, finding out about Jessica.'

It was heartfelt and genuine. What we all wanted was the safe return of those two innocents. Their loved things were all around us; reading books, their doll's houses, beloved, furry playthings and pretty dresses with frills and bows.

It was clear from their gaunt appearance that neither parent had been eating properly. Who could blame them?

I began to speak before deciding against it. *Where is Rhonda?* I wrote.

Candice answered. Her voice was quiet.

'She's been a treasure, yet she has her own family to care for. She's been visiting as much as she could. Funny. Although we weren't that close in school, she's been so supportive; more so than many of my other friends.

People surprise you, especially when terrible things happen.'

Her voice trailed off as she and Daniel joined hands.

'DC Frost . . . Kimberly,' he said. 'Just . . . please do your best to bring them back. Please.'

I nodded humbly.

'We all will,' DCI Aldershot added.

Mark then gently explained that I would be wearing a microphone when I met LM. That way he and the police could monitor the meeting. He also showed them a duplicate of the tracker in the attaché case.

Mr Bowen brought out the fifty thousand pounds from a safe in his study next door. He tipped it onto one of the beds. I doubted if any of us had ever seen that much cash at one time. Mark and Mr Bowen started to pack it carefully, with Mark checking that the bundles were all secured with currency straps.

Mark must have been agitated about the whole event, maybe about me too.

He dropped some bundles on the floor before Steven decided to take over. Once it was all packed, Mark checked the hidden transmitter was functioning. The case was closed with two final clicks.

How much money do you place on a child's life? It was inconceivable to be faced with a decision like that. What if the Bowens hadn't had that amount of available cash? What then?

That someone could be calculating and callous enough to exploit that parental love was simply disgusting. I hated this person more than I'd hated anyone — yet I now had to meet them, engage them in conversation and give them money they had no right to at all. Could I control my feelings? For the sake of Scarlett and Crystal, I had to.

★   ★   ★

At last, it was time to drive to the meeting place by the Wye River. We headed towards Ross-on-Wye south-east of Hereford, me sitting in the rear of the powerful BMW. What if it all went pear-shaped because of some action or inaction on my part? How could I live with myself after that?

LM had chosen the handover point well. There were open fields on both sides of the river and it was well away from any road, even a dirt track. There was a spruce forest about half a mile away in one direction, deciduous trees in the other.

The temperature was just above freezing with a wind from the east that made it feel much chillier. Outside the car, my nose twitched as my breaths formed tiny puffs of cloud. A mist swirled over the river, drifting to and fro at the whims of the December breeze.

I tugged up my anorak hood for some protection.

'He'll want to see your face to make sure it's you, Kimberly. Ditch the hood.' DS Cameron was right, so I pushed it back off. At least I could keep my woolly gloves on. Everything I did now was to please some high-profile villain's every caprice. There was no way I could alienate him.

'You'd best make a move,' Steven told me when he checked his watch. Mark was ostensibly listening from his own surveillance position. There was an ambulance on standby too — although I wasn't meant to have heard about that for obvious reasons.

I wiped my bad eye. No stab vest or weapon. Just yours truly in civvies; a jumper, coat, skirt, thick leggings and my long black boots. Oh, and carrying fifty thousand pounds in cash.

'Head to the bench over there by the water's edge, Kimberly.' Steven pointed at a dot in the distance. 'We'll drive off in case he's watching but we won't be far away. Good luck.'

There was no path across the grasslands between the road and the river. In places it was so muddy, my boots squelched as they stuck in the manky gunge, but most of it was frozen solid. My legs and boots were soon soaked from the tall grasses, though it was that vulnerable sensation being so alone and exposed that made me most uneasy. The case was becoming heavier with each step, plus my legs ached from the cold and effort of striding. Then it decided to begin sleeting.

'Great. Absholutely b . . . bloody great,' I muttered, moving to flip my hood up again before remembering Steven's words.

In the end, I reached the bench by the river. There was a more solid pathway, maybe for cyclists. I put down the case while I stood catching my breath.

The river flowed by, burbling in its churning, melodic way. A few brave ducks and coots swam within the reeds on the water's edge. The ducks began quacking in the hopes of food.

'Shut up, you shtupid birdsh,' I mumbled, feeling very apprehensive. My intermittent outbursts peppered with naughty words when I'd slipped in the mud and grasses made this unreal scenario real in a way. If Mark were listening, recording every sound, they were probably unintelligible in any case.

'Hope you're not the short of villain to keep a maiden waiting, Mr Lollipop Man,' were my next mutterings. He was late and it was so cold, I had begun to shiver.

He wasn't. From out of a treeline that butted up to the river, a trail bike roared towards me. He was by my side in moments, the choking fumes from the motor catching in my throat. His features were covered by a helmet with darkened visor. The leathers and helmet were a dull black. No Hell's Angel insignia, nor any other identifying mark. The bike was actually a Harley, with no number plate to track. I mentally noted the model number and colour for all the good it would do.

'You that Kimberly copper?' he asked.

I faced him, my dark chocolate hair

covered with specks of melting white-ness. The sleet was now obscuring the view of the forests that were now a smoke-grey haze.

'Yeah. I can see your ugly face now. Come here. Open your jacket.'

I did, wondering what was going on.

'Now undo that shiny blouse of yours.'

'No. Itsh too cold.' I raised my voice.

'Open it, or I will.'

Slowly, I complied, unbuttoning my top. The cold was nothing compared to the humiliation and shame I felt.

He reached out to grab the micro-phone nestled in my cleavage, then yanked it free of the attached straps taped to my body. They cut into my back before snapping. He flung the device into the river.

I gasped. Now I had no chance to call for help. My prayers were that my colleagues were still watching with binoculars.

'Go on. Cover yourself up, lady. You're not my type, certainly with that misshapen mug of yours.' He began chuckling then stopped suddenly. 'Open the case. Hurry up.'

I did as he asked. He must have suspected I'd been wearing a wire. What about the case?

'Lovely.' He lifted a bundle up and flipped through it. Was he checking if it was blank sheets of paper instead of real money? More likely he was savouring his moment of triumph.

'The girlsh?' I asked him.

'Oh, those brats. We'll release them in a couple of hours like what I told you.'

The motorcyclist then scooped the bundles of cash out of the case, into the saddlebags slung over his bike. Inwardly, I groaned. Now we had no chance of tracking the ransom and this man.

To me, it was obvious he wasn't the Lollipop Man. LM was intelligent and calculating, not a clown like this character.

'We . . . what now?' I asked.

'I make my getaway, of course. I

know your copper pals are watching me right now, so I need to give 'em summat else to think about.'

At those words, he drew a gun from inside his zipped-up jacket. I shuddered as he pointed it at my stomach.

Hell, I thought. *He's going to shoot me.*

My heart began pumping madly as my throat went dry. Adrenalin was coursing through every part of my body ready to fight or run. Neither of those were possibilities. He was too far away to attack. I'd be dead before I reached him.

'Pu . . . Pleashe don't shoot me,' I pleaded, backing towards the fast-flowing river.

The gunman stepped forward, just as we heard the faint sound of a car engine starting in the distance. The police? They'd be far too late.

'Say your prayers, lady.'

He raised the weapon further, aiming for my chest, gripping it with both hands.

Desperately, I stumbled back trying to reduce the size of my body by cringing. One step . . . two . . . He'd backed me up to the river bank.

The uneven soil collapsed beneath my feet. I flailed my arms desperately trying to regain my balance. No good. I tumbled back into the swiftly flowing ripples that were undercutting the bend where I'd stood. Frigid waters engulfed me, whisking me from the riverside.

Mouthfuls of churning water choked me. My feet kicked downwards, trying to gain some purchase on the river bottom. It was far too deep. My clothing was soaked, chilling me to my bones. I had to swim back as fast as I could.

Above the sound of ducks, there was the noise of my assailant speeding away. There was a good chance I'd survive if I could swim to the shore. But something was wrong. It wasn't working. I was sinking.

My clothing was saturated, weighing me down. Water filled my mouth again as I struggled to the surface, shrugging off my anorak and cardigan. A gasp of air. The waters closed over my head.

Those damn boots. There was nothing more I could do.

Mark, I thought. *Save me.*

But he wasn't there. No one was. Looking up there was dull skylight, below was only darkness . . . the darkness of my grave.

8

I was drowning. All around was greyness. I had to breathe . . .

'Good girl,' said a voice from above. I spluttered, then sat up gasping for air. Or at least I tried. Firm hands held me down gently, turning my head to the side.

'Go on, Kimberly. Get it all out. That's it.'

Foul-tasting water spewed from my mouth and throat. There was grass next to my face.

'Shteven?' I spluttered. I saw him kneeling in front of my face. He was soaking too.

'You shaved me?'

He smiled, before quickly comprehending there was something wrong.

'Quick. Give me your overcoat. She's hypothermic. Damn. Where are the paramedics?'

I could hear a siren in the distance. DCI Aldershot covered me as best he could. The hairs of the coat brushed one side of my face.

'She's not shivering.'

'Yeah. That's bad. Shivering is a defence mechanism to help warm you up. She's way past that.' I could barely sense his hands massaging my skin.

'Start rubbing her limbs. Hard. Her circulation's shutting down.'

A fog seemed to descend over my mind. Vague sounds mingled as other sirens approached.

'Thermal blankets,' one duck called out. 'Get those wet clothes off.'

'Warm saline drip,' another quacked.

'Talkin' ducksh,' I mumbled in my delirium.

'No. Don't let her doze off. Kimberly!' A slap. 'Wake up, Kimberly.' Another slap. Was this Donald or Daffy?

'I's avake,' I mumbled again.

'Talk to me, Kimberly. That's an order.'

'Yuz a duck. Can't order . . . '

'Kimberly!'

'Don't shout, Dazzy, I can hear you.'

All around men and women were staring down at me. My body was lifted as we moved bumpety, bump, bump, just like in the story book Dad used to read me.

I began to recite it word for word, oblivious to the ministrations of the ambulance crew. It's probably what saved my life.

★   ★   ★

After I don't know how long, I opened one eye. A nurse peered down at me before removing the tape on the other. It was clear that I was in hospital. One of the nurses had been helping Mum a few days before. I recognised her multi-hued hair.

Steven was there. He was covered in a reflective foil blanket, as was I.

'Roasht duck,' I muttered.

'What did she say?' Steven asked the nurse.

'My guess is that you look like a duck ready for the oven. Actually, I agree with her. I'll get some orange sauce from the canteen,' she joked.

'So, her mind's intact? Thank goodness. Thought we lost you for a bit, Kimberly. It was touch and go.'

Pulling my hand from under the blankets, I reached out to him. 'You shaved me. Thank you.'

'Good thing I do endurance swims in the winter. Even so, that water was bad news.'

At that point, I recalled we'd lost our suspect as well as all of that money.

'How long? Girlsh?'

'Almost four hours. No sign of the little ones, and before you ask, the biker made his getaway.'

I felt sick. It had all been for nothing.

'Mark? Ishy here?'

'Mark? No. 'Fraid not. Busy.'

That told me a great deal about the relationship that now existed between us. I'd pushed him away. Rightly or wrongly, what we'd had was ended. He

170

must have realised what had happened to me, especially since he'd been listening when it all went pear-shaped.

'The guy on the motorcycle . . . he was aware of all our plans; the mike you wore, the bug in the bag. He must have found out from one of us. It's just too much of a coincidence.' He paused before coming closer. 'Just how much can you trust your mate?'

I sat up, astounded. 'You shaying Mark . . . ?'

'Is the mole. Yes. The only other people who had all the information were the DCI, you, me and the Bowens. Clearly, they're not involved. So that leaves the only one that none of us has met until this week . . . apart from you.'

I considered all the facts. Coincidence wasn't out of the question. If I were accepting a ransom, I'd check for a wire. Also, he couldn't put an attaché bag on the bike, could he?

OK. Mark and I may have our issues — but he would never be a part of anything criminal — especially my murder.

'Not Mark,' I told Steven with as much conviction as I could.

Steven didn't respond. Minutes after that, DCI Aldershot came in. He smiled at me before his frown returned and came over while the nurse took my blood pressure.

'Good to see you're awake, Kimberly. We were so worried. I should have done more to protect you. As it stands, we lost the money but more importantly to us, we almost lost you. That's something I will have to live with all my life.'

He turned to Steven.

'But we have a much bigger problem than the girls not being released. Mark Rathaway is missing, along with two of my officers. The van they were using to monitor the drop has gone and we've not heard a word from them despite numerous attempts to contact them on the radio. I'm extremely concerned and — dare I say it — given the fiasco of that money exchange, I now believe Mark Rathaway has betrayed us all.'

Hurriedly, I printed my message for him to read. *There must be another reason. I trust Mark. There's no way he could overcome two police officers on his own.*

'Who said he was on his own? Possibly the guy who almost drowned you — ' Steven began, just as there was a knock on the door of my private room. I imagined an officer was on guard outside.

My DS went to answer it. I could hear the conversation outside in the corridor.

'There's a guy downstairs insisting he see you, DS Cameron. Shall I ask the front desk to send him up?'

Steven's deep voice replied.

'Could be a reporter. Do we have a name?'

There was a pause and a mumbled conversation. I gathered that Steven agreed. Moments later he returned — with my Mark by his side, panting.

The chief became quite angry on seeing him.

'Where have you been, Rathaway? And where are my two officers?'

Mark glanced over to me. He was out of breath but managed a reassuring smile on seeing I was awake and OK.

'The constables are fine. I left them in Much Dewchurch keeping an eye on the ransom guy,' he managed to blurt out in between gasps. He'd obviously been running.

'What? You've found him?'

Mark nodded, putting his hands on his knees and stooping over.

'How? Where have you been? Answer me, man.' The DCI was fit to be roped.

'Excuse me, sir. I'll answer all your questions . . . but first I need . . . you to order your armed officers to this address. He has a gun. We can't let him get away.'

The head of the investigation took one long look at the state of Mark, then at the paper he held out, before lifting the radio off his chest.

'No!' screamed Mark. 'Not radio. Telephone. We — dear Lord — we have to keep radio silence. I . . . think he has a police scanner. Listening to our communications.' He staggered. By this time my nurse had realised he was in distress. She'd pressed the Emergency buzzer.

'Ashma 'tack,' I said. I should have realised it sooner. He'd had a few when he was a youth, though I'd never actually seen them before. He'd told me he'd grown out of them. Clearly, he was mistaken.

Steven helped him sit down while our chief presumably went to phone for the Armed Response team to go to the address, about fifteen minutes from us.

The doctor who'd run in adminis-tered some spray into his mouth, told him to breathe through the nose, and slow his breathing. It was remarkable how quickly it worked. We all needed to hear what Mark had to say. At last he stood up.

'Shall we go get this guy? I'll fill you in on the way. Can you come too, Kimberly? Payback would be good considering what he did to you. I heard it all on the police radio in the van.'

I turned to the doctor.

'Blood pressure, temperature and heart rate are all normal, Miss Frost. You're free to go,' the nurse announced. The DCI nodded too.

I sat up, tossing the silvered blanket to one side. A quick change of clothing and I'd be ready to join them —

'Kimberly!' Mark shouted.

The three guys immediately turned away as the nurse rushed over to cover me.

'Some privacy please. gentlemen. Will you wait outside? Now.'

Talk about closing the barn door after the horse had bolted. How utterly, utterly embarrassing. At least they could have put some clothing on me when I'd been recovering.

★ ★ ★

176

Back in the chief's BMW, DS Cameron was driving with the chief talking to the officer-in-charge of the armed response unit by mobile phone. They'd taken up positions around a caravan park on the outskirts on Much Dewchurch. Furthermore, contact had been made with the two other officers who had been keeping surveillance on the house for the past four hours.

Mark sat with me in the back seat. Chief Aldershot hung up, then turned to Mark.

'So help me, Rathaway, if this is a wild duck chase . . . ' I wasn't sure if he meant goose, or was deliberately reminding me of my duck nightmare.

'It isn't, sir. I'd put another tracker inside one of the money bundles. Very small.'

When could he have done that, I wondered? Replaying events, I recalled the dropped bundles in the Bowens' home. He must have slipped one in then.

'Why not tell us?' my chief asked,

clearly a little aggrieved.

'Precautions. As it worked out, I was right. We would have lost him otherwise.' He paused. 'The tech officers and I were monitoring it all in that unmarked police van. I told them not to call it in, so you can blame me. It made sense for the thief to be listening in on the police bands. I would, if I was picking up all that cash illegally. None of the techies had a mobile phone, and mine was flat.

'We tracked him to Much Dewchurch and saw him parking his bike at the back of one of the caravans — an old green one by an oak tree. Then we watched him carry the saddlebags with the money inside. He's not budged since.'

DCI Aldershot considered that.

'You left the officers there and came back to Hereford. How did you get there without a car?'

Mark smiled, apologetically.

'Ran. Hitch-hiked . . . Overdid the exercise bit. I knew if I rang you from some house along the way, you wouldn't believe me. You probably thought I was mixed up with him, disappearing like that.'

'The thought did cross our minds, Mr Rathaway. I'm glad we were wrong.'

The chief turned to Steven, who'd been driving.

'Almost there. We'll pull up around the corner. Don't want to spook him — especially if the children are inside with him.'

The DCI dialled a number on the phone.

'Are your team ready, Commander? No sign of movement from the van? Excellent.'

We turned a corner to see some armed officers already deployed. The senior officer waved us down, and the two ranking officers left us in the car to confer about the next step.

There was an uncomfortable silence. At last, Mark spoke.

'You OK, Kimberly?'

I took out pen and paper. *I don't*

plan on going swimming in a river any time soon, if that's what you mean. DS Cameron saved me.

It was odd to talk about it without bursting into tears. I'd almost died, for Heaven's sake. I actually thought I had. No white light at the end of the tunnel, though.

There was time enough to let my emotions take over. As for the anger I was feeling about this stranger who'd tried to end my life, even that was suppressed right now. All I wanted was to see him arrested and those girls to be found safe.

Steven dashed back and gave us an encrypted radio. Even with a scanner, the motorcyclist wouldn't hear what was going on.

'Don't press 'Speak' whatever you do. We don't want the team distracted. Just listen. You deserve to hear it as it happens.'

He disappeared back to the mobile command post with the others. I began to shiver as the car heater was turned off. The clothing the nurse had brought me wasn't all that warm.

Mark noticed. Awkwardly he took off his thick fleece and passed it to me. I struggled into it, feeling better almost immediately.

'Shmells,' I said without thinking.

'Sorry,' he apologised, pushing his glasses up to the bridge of his nose.

'No. Did not mean that. Shmells nice. Of you.'

'I wanted to come and save you, Kimberly,' he blurted out. 'I could hear it all; the chief calling for back-up, your screams from the water, Steven diving in . . . we were so far away, but we heard it all. It was the hardest thing I've ever done not to rush back to be with you. But a part of me kept saying *What would Kimberly want?* And the answer was, '*Track the ransom guy down . . . Save Scarlett and Crystal.* I'm so sorry.'

'Mark. I'm alive and you f . . . *found* 'im. I'sh p . . . pr . . . *proud* of you.'

Up ahead, the armed officers in their

protective gear were deploying. I couldn't see the target caravan; it was around another corner. As if on cue, the encrypted police radio squawked to life. Like our bosses standing outside in the cold afternoon gloom, we listened, almost entranced, as the officers slowly tightened their noose around the suspect's hideout.

Based on what he'd said, the children might be held elsewhere, though there would surely be some clues as to their whereabouts.

I heard the team commander say 'Go. Go. Go' and the noise of doors being opened, followed by concussion charges meant to disorient whoever was in there. I reminded myself he had a gun.

Crisp calls of 'Clear' indicated that they'd met no resistance checking each room inside. 'Weapon found and secured,' then 'Subject one secured.' At last, having checked all the rooms presumably, the ranking officer announced. 'All clear. All clear.'

From start to finish, it took less than fifteen seconds. Those armed officers knew their stuff.

'Any sign of the missing girls?' DCI Aldershot asked, unable to contain his anxiety any longer.

The reply sent a cold shiver through every cell of my body.

'There's a female. She's in a bad state. Ambulance required.'

★   ★   ★

Knowing that all was secure inside, the four of us entered the old static caravan. By now it was quite dark. Other police vehicles were arriving including forensics and a truck with a generator and large floodlamps for illuminating the outside. We were grateful there was no rain or snow. Wearing gloves, we all went through to where the motorcyclist was lying on his front, arms cuffed behind him.

The paramedics were having a busy day. His wife or girlfriend had been found in a bedroom. No one had been caring for her and she was severely malnourished.

My assailant had been given his rights when we arrived. One armed officer, his visor raised, stood nonchalantly with his firearm resting across his stomach, held casually in both hands. They were taking no chances. Two other officers were collecting the money still in bundles on the table. A half-full bottle of whisky was next to the cash.

'This is Guy Burtenshaw according to his passport. We're checking his rap sheet now, sir.'

The ranking firearms officer had been busy, it seemed.

Guy sneered when he saw us. There was a cut and some bruises on his face.

'Resisted arrest,' the officer stated when he noticed the Chief Inspector raise a quizzical eyebrow.

'Did he now? Nasty little piece of garbage then, Sergeant. Pity he wasn't more of a problem.'

It was hardly a cryptic statement.

I understood that the policeman's attitude was partially due to this Burtenshaw character almost killing me. His involvement in this crime against innocent children was another factor. In my limited experience, one thing that united our force was the desire to protect innocents. I was sure it was the same with all police.

'Surprised to see you here, Ugly Puss,' he said, on seeing me. 'Enjoy your swim?'

I didn't respond. Staring at his scruffy, unshaven face, I understood he was one of life's losers. This place said it all. He was nothing.

'What about the weapon?' Steven asked.

'Replica. A very good one but no threat, sir,' the constable standing guard responded.

That made me feel sick and relieved at the same time. I walked away so the man in cuffs couldn't see me. Mark was in another room. He was probably searching the computer we'd seen when we entered. As for Guy Burtenshaw, he could not have shot me — yet his empty threats had almost ended my life.

'Where are the girls?' Steven asked the prisoner. I came back in, pulling Mark's fleece tighter around me in the chilly room.

Burtenshaw laughed. 'No idea, coppers. And I ain't this Lollipop geezer either. He had no intention of returning the rug-rats but he reckoned that ransom rubbish would get you piggies running around. He posted the photo through my door during the night and told me to pretend to be him. We'd split the money but it weren't important to him at all. He's got what he wants and that's it.'

'What does he want?' the Chief Inspector asked.

'Gawd, you're thick. He's already got what he wants. Those girls will never be found, least not alive. Revenge on the parents — that's what.'

As we began to leave, he shouted out.

186

'Sorry. There is one other thing he wants.'

We all turned to stare at him on the floor.

'What's that?' the Chief asked.

'Miss Ugly Puss. He wants her dead.'

★   ★   ★

Walking to the car was hard. I almost stumbled twice, unable to concentrate on anything but those final words.

'Don't let him upset you,' Steven said in a fatherly tone as he steadied me. 'It's a pathetic attempt to regain control of his situation. Come on, Kimberly. You're stronger than that.'

I began sobbing.

'Thash just it. I'm not . . . not any more. Had enough. I w . . . want to resign.'

'From the case? No need. You're already on leave.'

I stopped and made him face me, the chilled December winds numbing my face.

187

'Not from thish case. From the police.'

9

This week had been a nightmare, today especially. Whatever self-confidence I'd had was now gone.

A uniformed officer kindly drove me home. I didn't recognise her. Possibly she was my replacement but right now I didn't care. She tried to engage me in conversation but after a few polite one-word answers, she gave up. I wasn't in a talking mood. I wasn't in the mood for anything.

My face was a mess, no love life and I'd verbally resigned from the Force. Oh, and let's not forget some psychopathic kidnapper who wanted to kill me. I prayed resigning would make him change his mind, as I wouldn't be a threat any longer.

Dad was right to think this job was too dangerous.

It seemed that someone, probably

Mark, had phoned ahead to explain the situation. Dad and Mum came out as the car stopped in the driveway. Mrs Dawling's curtains across the road twitched. I gave her a wave; a tiny attempt to tell her to mind her own business.

My parents fussed around. It was oppressive and demeaning but, remembering being alone in Cygnet Place, I appreciated being cosseted.

Following a long, hot shower and shampoo to remove the detritus from the River Wye, I spent the remainder of the evening on the settee in my dressing gown. Misty snuggled up next to me. He'd always been my cat.

Together, we watched some mindless television shows. It was only when I realised I was half way through an episode of *The Bill* that I stood up, turned the telly off and went to see what we were having for tea. Misty padded alongside.

There were voices in the porch. I went to see who it was, waiting out of sight in the dining room. Mum and Dad were talking quietly to someone.

'No, Mark. We don't think it's a good idea. She's in some sort of shutdown mode. Never seen her like this. We'll tell her you called, OK?'

The front door opened and closed gently. My parents came back in.

'Do you think she'll be OK, Ted?'

Dad's reply was more muted.

'I don't have an answer, Linda.' Then there was the sound of my father crying. It was a sound I'd never heard before.

★   ★   ★

Friday was the fifteenth, though it felt more like the thirteenth to me, heavy with potential disasters. For starters, Misty had scampered in front of me twice in the hour I'd been up. And I'd cracked my compact mirror in a fit of frustration when I'd thrown it to the floor. Did cracked mirrors give the same number of years of bad luck as

191

broken ones? Those nightmares about blinking ducks hadn't helped either.

'What's the point?' I moaned to Dad. He'd been to work early to arrange the day there, yet he'd insisted on coming back to pester me about keeping my physiotherapy appointment.

Mum had taken the car down to the Co-op. Christmas shopping, she'd said. I was, glad she was better, but that didn't shift my moody blues.

I wasn't properly dressed, but so what?

'The ph . . . physio won't work. 'Sides, it's a long drive in. I'm not up to it.'

'Come on. This isn't like you, kitten.'

I put my answer in the notebook. It was filling up quickly. *Getting myself almost drowned taught me a few things, Dad. Almost dying isn't what I signed up for with the cops. You were right all along. I should have listened to you. Someone else will have to find the girls. I'm going to formally resign before Christmas. Or maybe today. No*

192

point putting it off.

My father read it carefully before replying, his voice dropping an octave as he stood up over me.

'Yesterday must have been horrific for you in that river. We can't imagine what you went through. Nonetheless, I was wrong about the police and you. I told you that once and I don't like repeating myself. What you did yesterday to help save those girls was heroic. You had no idea what danger you'd face giving him the ransom.'

He took a deep breath. Speaking so deeply was hard for him but he was doing his best to get me to realise something important.

'Kimberly Tabitha Frost. You're a grown woman and whatever you choose to do, we'll respect that. What you do about your job, that's your choice even though your mother and I think you're a great detective. But one thing's for sure, young lady. You're keeping that hospital appointment today, even if I have to drag you there myself. No arguments. Or else.'

I tried to grin. Dad's Mr Grumpy voice never worked on me, but he was right about today. I had an appointment and people were expecting me to be there. The fact that he'd offered to take me was good, because it was true, I did not feel up to that drive. Every muscle in my body ached and I hadn't had much calm sleep, despite the sedative Dr Little had prescribed.

'You w . . . win,' I conceded. 'Just don't take me to f . . . feed any ducksh on the w . . . way.'

★   ★   ★

There were occasional drifts of snow by the roadside as Dad drove me to Hereford. My attention was elsewhere, on the scenery. Even in winter, Hereford was beautiful; fields and hedges and far too many of what Mark called 'sheeps'. I'd often wondered why our county was renowned for its cattle

194

with so many woolly beasts everywhere.

Kylie and Jason were singing *Especially For You* on Radio 2, Dad's choice of station. That reminded me — I'd promised Mark's niece I'd go with them to Worcester on Sunday to see Santa. The poor girl had been saddled with the name Kylie just like so many girls had, after that *Neighbours* wedding back in 1988.

For a few seconds, I'd been day-dreaming but then I recalled Scarlett and Crystal. There'd be no visit from Santa for them — even if they were alive. What was it Burtenshaw said about Lollipop Man? He wanted to keep the girls?

I shook my head. I wasn't involved any longer. It was up to other police now. Maybe Burtenshaw had told my former colleagues where or who he was, but I doubted he knew. LM was too clever.

We reached the hospital car park where Dad gave me a box that had been on the back seat.

'Early present for Christmas. Thought it might help you feel better about yourself.'

I lifted out two heavy metal rings. Wonder Woman's bullet deflecting bracelets — adult size. Dad must have made me a new set.

I put them on, then pulled my jumper over them. They were cold and snug, but wearing them reminded me of that super-heroine wannabe I once was. I gave a lopsided smile.

'Thanksh Dad.' I gave him a hug. Wonder Woman might have suffered a temporary setback, yet she was there inside me still.

He was heading off to Monmouth for some meeting with a car parts manufacturer; a new lucrative contract to be signed. We arranged a time and place for me to be picked up later.

I'd found some tinted glasses to wear to hide my bad eye and I'd become a dab hand at hiding my sagging mouth unobtrusively behind one of my brightly coloured scarves.

Making my way through the corridors to the Physiotherapy area, I glanced around at who was there. Old habits, I guessed. A young teenager struggling to walk within the parallel bars, someone doing step-ups and two ladies doing muscle strengthening exercises with hand grips, one of them with her arm in a sling.

At that point, I spied the man from the other day, the one who was quite familiar. This time, he was easy to place. Gareth Gisburn — he'd been in some television shows, plus ads in newspapers and magazines. He was seated at a desk, presumably to speak to the staff.

Mum always said she fancied him, almost as much as Dad. Could I be cheeky enough to ask for an autograph?

Then I remembered where we were and why I was here. Not with this face, I couldn't.

An older nurse came over as I took my seat by the magnetometer. She wasn't one I'd seen before. She gave me a smile, though I couldn't return the greeting, not properly.

Even though I was taking a steroid called Prednisolone for the inflammation, the magnetometer gave me more hope. A machine like my dad's factory built was more credible than some miracle pill, I supposed.

Gareth must have noticed as he came over. The nurse excused herself to get my notes.

'Hello, Miss. Hope you don't mind a total stranger talking to you, but I promise I'm not trying to chat you up.'

''Sh all right.' He was even more handsome in person, even though he was around forty. His voice had that posh Nigel Havers accent, even though he lived nearby according to super-fan Mum.

'You have Bell's Palsy.' As a chat up line it was right up there with *Did it hurt when you fell out of Heaven?* Suddenly he wasn't Mr Drop-Dead-Gorgeous any more — even though he continued as though he wasn't upsetting me.

'Doesn't look too bad. Did it just happen?' Cheeky guy. It wasn't as though he was a nurse or a doctor. His only qualification was as a bit of male eye-candy.

'Yesh,' was my less than polite reply.

'You're that detective . . . the one on the Bowen girl case?'

I was becoming impatient to start my treatment.

'Nursh?' I called out. She replied that she'd be a moment. I turned to my annoying companion. 'Yesh again, if you must know.'

'I admire you, Miss. And just to put your mind at rest, this Bell's Palsy isn't all bad. It allowed me to see what's important in my life.'

I examined those famous features. The smile wasn't quite perfect and the eyelid drooped a smidgen.

'You had thish?'

'Don't be so surprised. It can affect anyone — even superstars like me,' He laughed, giving me a wink to show he was being sarcastic about the superstar thing. I'd seen him on *Good Morning Britain* and he was so down to earth then.

'Shorry to be rude. How long?'

'Six weeks. Showed me who my friends really are. Finished with modelling and celeb status now, even if they would employ me again. Not for photo-shoots. That ship has well and truly sunk. Had a game show offer yesterday. Turned it down. I was a teacher in a former life. I might go back to it . . . do some meaningful work for a change.'

'But I shore you lasht w . . . we . . . week.'

'Pre-recorded. By the way, my palsy was worse — although your speech sounds unusually bad. Your eyebrow does twitch.

'I've had my last session with Honey-Bun here.' He tapped the magnetometer. 'Just came in today to be signed off. This beautiful little gadget will sort you out, Miss.'

'Name'sh . . . ' I wrote it down. Too hard to say.

'Kimberly. Beautiful name. And I'm . . . '

'Gareth.' I grinned as well as I could. Then I remembered. 'Autograph pleashe? F . . . for Mum.'

I understood what he'd been saying. Already I could see how short-sighted I'd been. Hurtful too.

'Any advishe?' I asked.

'Mouth exercises and massages five times a day. It might feel like you're a baby learning to speak for the first time but, believe me, it pays off. I've accepted that my face will never be the same as it was. Others might not notice but I do.'

A nurse was approaching, a technician by her side. Gareth shook my hand and gave me a card.

'My details. Give me a ring. Bring your mum around if you like. My wife would love to meet you both. As for you, Kimberly, get yourself better soon.

Those missing kids need you.'

'But my f . . . face?'

'They don't need your good looks, Detective. They need your brains.'

I nodded. Amazingly, resigning was suddenly no longer an option.

The nurse began to set me up with Honey-Bun for my half-hour session. It would be boring sitting here. Then I recalled the shopping bag Dad had packed with a crossword magazine and some book with some new Japanese puzzles. Sudoko, I think Dad called it. Whatever, it was worth a look. Pity I didn't have those notes about the girls to study.

Opening the bag, I chuckled. Good old Dad. There were no puzzle books; only a thick folder about the investigation. The sneaky so-and-so. Honey-Bun began her hypnotic humming and I began to read.

★　★　★

My father drove me home. His meeting with the client had been productive. I was much chattier than I'd been this morning, though I doubted Dad understood most of my ramblings. The skies were brighter, the sheep were whiter and as for the future . . . I'd have to wait and see.

Back in Bromyard, I joined Mum in making a fresh batch of mince pies. Her cough was gone, her paleness replaced by rosy cheeks.

Because Mark was busy working, it gave me some freedom to think about us, without dealing with him in person. How could I have possibly missed all the signs? In my head, I reviewed what I knew about Mark and his love life. He'd hardly had any girlfriends as such. There was Mandy, or was it Sandy? Three years ago? And that had only lasted a few months.

And then there was me. None of the guys I'd been romantically involved with had ever been as much fun to be around as he had. Most had been clones of that tall, dark and good-looking fantasy I'd always had. Was I so shallow that I'd automatically fallen in love with a man simply because of his looks? The upsetting answer was . . . yes. I felt so degraded thinking it.

Not that my Mark wasn't good-looking. Without those unflattering glasses and with a decent haircut, he was quite rugged. He was intelligent and had a dry sense of humour that I loved.

I'd been rude to him yesterday — totally out of order. No excuses, especially that easy cop-out that he'd understand for what it was. Yeah . . . just like I'd understood when that low-life Barry had told me to get lost.

I considered that point. Mark had always lived by that tenet *Do unto others as you'd have them do to you.*

Barry was more *Do unto others . . . then split.*

My apology to Mark would be hard for me. The words in my head came out either too insincere or too formal. Every attempt was wrong. Maybe if I wrote it down so as not to stumble under unpronounceable phrases? Should I give him a mince pie with cream first of all, to soften him up? He was a big fan of Christmas; carols, twinkly lights and all those irritating Christmas pop songs which drove me mad for two months before.

Mum opened another jar of mince-meat, poured it into the mixing bowl, then emptied the last of the brandy bottle into it.

'It's too dry without it,' Mum said by way of justification.

'I believe you, Mum.' Then I had a thought. 'Can I make a big one, p . . . pleashe?'

★ ★ ★

Mark came over after work. It was obvious he'd been home and changed. There was no possibility that he'd wear a reindeer jumper with a lit-up nose along with a red hat on for his day job. Then again, my Mark was never one for conventions.

I saw him through my frost-covered bedroom window as he approached our front door. I'd expected him half an hour before. Why can't men be punctual?

I watched as he took his glasses off for some reason, promptly dropped them into a pool of water then frantically tried to dry them on, you guessed it, his new jumper. Typical Mark.

He glanced around to see if anyone had noticed. Just me and Mrs Dawling across the road.

Our doorbell began playing *Frosty The Snowman*. Dad must have put a Christmas-themed one in.

'I'll get it,' I shouted, bounding downstairs. My words came out sounding surprisingly normal.

'I wonder who that could possibly be?' Mum commented. Ignoring her, I opened our garland-festooned door to enter the porch. Mark stood outside, Santa hat and all.

'Oh, itsh only you. Come to shee Dad?'

I let him in, keeping my happy face concealed.

Mark removed his hat as the doorbell started up again with *Frosty*. The damn bell push had stuck. Mark reached out to fix it.

'Listen, Kimberly,' he said to my back. 'I told you I was sorry. I still want to be your friend even if I can't be any more than that. What do you say?'

In reply, I turned and gave him my giant mince pie on a plate along with a generous dollop of cream. I kept my face impassive.

'Minch tart?' Tart was easier to say than pie.

'Kimberly. I haven't taken my jacket off yet and my glasses are still dripping. Give a bloke a chance, will you?'

Then he noticed the writing on the mega-pie.

'What's this? *3WSSIK*?'

Damn. What was it with men? I turned the plate around.

'*KISS ME*?' he read out.

'If you insisht,' I replied before taking

the plate, putting it down then pressing
my lips to his.

10

Hesitantly at first, Mark enfolded me in his arms. Our lips met.

As we parted, he asked how it was.

'Cold and w . . . wet. Shall we try it again?'

Ever the gallant knight in soggy armour, he did his best. We were about to attempt a third time, when I espied Mum staring at us, grinning happily.

'Thish ish not a spectator sport,' I admonished.

'Sorry, Kimberly. I just might suggest you allow the poor man to take his coat and gloves off first before attacking him. Now you're both soaking.'

I laughed, having to dab my mouth in frustration.

'I don't mind. Do you, Mark?'

As he hung his coat and scarf up, Mum asked if he'd had his dinner yet.

It was late but I'd requested we wait until he came, which didn't go down well with Dad, who was a creature of habit.

'Er . . . no, as a matter of fact,' he replied.

'We'd love you to join us. Especially Kimberly. Ted, will you give us a hand in the kitchen?'

'About time, Kimberly. I'm starving.' Dad came past us, grumbling.

I was eager to tell Mark everything and give him a proper apology for my attitude yesterday. I took his still-clammy hand in mine.

'Just explain something to me, Kimberly. I assume we're friends again but those kisses . . . What does that mean?'

'It meansh . . . ' No. Words were too hard to say. I began scribbling in my book.

It means that I would like to be your girlfriend. Really, really like. All this palsy and nearly dying . . . it's made me realise I've been a prat, not seeing what's right in front of me. No guarantees but let's see how it goes. Slowly.

Mark read my note.

'Slowly? Those kisses?'

Apology kisses. The proper ones will happen when I sort this face . . . My pen was running out.

He nodded. 'That's fantastic. Can I have my mince pie now? Just 'cause that kissing made me tired. I need sugar.'

'You're joking, right? Dinner f . . . first. Tart after.'

★   ★   ★

Dinner was late but delicious. Eating was still messy for me, and drinking wine from my toddler's training mug wasn't very classy. I listened rather than doing a lot of talking.

Strangely it wasn't too disconcerting, eating like I was in front of Mark. He seemed to be very sensitive to the situation, and it was like old times hearing him and my parents in lively conversation.

Mum suggested that Mark and his family come around for Christmas. That would be a lot, even for our reasonably large dining room. There would be him, his mum and dad and Kylie. Mark's older sister was spending Christmas with her fiancé.

Mark agreed, after checking with his mother. Our families were old friends, after all.

We finished with mince pies for everyone. Mark agreed to split his enormous tart with me.

Mum and Dad retired to watch a taped episode of *Stars In Their Eyes*. We cleared the table, then I led Mark back to the dining room.

I turned off the normal lights so we could sit in the semi-darkness with the Christmas lights.

'Kissing time again?' he asked, his shadowy face coming close to mine.

'No. Mushy time is over, Mark. Whash ha . . . going on with the Bowen case?'

The look of disappointment on his lovely face made me reconsider. Pity he wore those ugly glasses. A makeover was essential before too long. Wire rims? Contacts, even?

'OK. Jush one.'

This time was less rushed and more loving. I sat back smiling a very satisfied Cheshire cat smile . . . at least inside.

'OK. Update on the kidnapping. That man who forced you into the river. He . . . what's the expression? He has form. Extortion, robbery with menace. He's quite proud to be involved in this high-profile case. Reckons he'll be a big shot in jail. Ended up singing like a budgie at the station.'

'Canary,' I corrected him, amused.

'Yeah. He told us he was contacted by Lollipop Man to do this ransom thing. Another distraction, just like Ted — your dad — said. The arrangement was, he'd keep half for doing the dirty work.'

'What he did almosh made me quit.'

'Well, Kimberly, he's up for some

pretty serious charges including attempted murder of a police officer. As for him thinking he'll be respected in prison, Steven told me he's in for a shock.'

I nodded. Other crims weren't too friendly to those who hurt children.

'W . . . what about the identity of LM?'

'He had no idea. Funny voice on the phone. They never met. That's the bizarrest thing. It transpires that there are contact mags for criminals. Need a cat burglar, a fence, a heavy? There are ads with CVs and testimonials, even pictures of victims to show their skills. We passed details onto Scotland Yard. Should result in a few arrests — but it doesn't help you guys.'

He sighed, letting his shoulders slump as he removed his glasses to rub his eyes. I guessed he'd been doing his best via the computer.

'Another dead end — no closer to finding the girls. It's a week now and all the police have to show for it is the arrests of three accomplices.'

I could sense Mark's frustration. In his new consultancy role, he was now identifying with the police. His younger sister wasn't much older than Crystal. One of those family situations when Mark and his other sister were well into their teens before his mum found herself pregnant with Kylie. Mrs Rathaway was now in her fifties with signs of rheumatoid arthritis. Having an energetic seven-year-old was hard work for her.

'You shtill taking Kylie shopping tomorrow?' I asked out of the blue.

'Yeah. She's been excited about seeing Father Christmas all week. It'd be great if you could come too. She loves to be with you. Plus, we could make a day of it, the three of us. Give Mum a break. Kylie's a bit of a handful at times and Dad's away at a conference all this weekend.'

Yesterday I'd decided to hide away, but I was still me inside. If Mark wanted me there, that was fine. As

Gareth had told me — other people might be unable to deal with a person who can't smile properly, but that was their problem, not mine.

People in wheelchairs, with limbs missing or who are blind; anyone who's different gets a second look. Being on the receiving end would be difficult — yet I could manage it, with Mark by my side.

'I'd love to come,' was my sincere reply.

★　★　★

Saturday morning arrived. Mark and Kylie were early, but I was ready. It was evident Mark had forewarned Kylie about my appearance.

Her first question after the usual welcome hug was, 'Does it hurt, Aunty?' She touched my cheek with her fingertips.

'No . . . maybe a little near my earsh. And I have to use drops in my eyesh or they get dry.'

'I'm sorry you're sick, Aunty Kimberly. Mark told me he kissed you. I'm really, really sorry he did that you. It's so yukky.' Then Kylie giggled. 'Guess what, Aunty Kimberly. We're all going to see Santa. And maybe Rudolph too.'

'Yesh. I'm coming as well.'

Mark was taking us to Worcester. It was about the same distance from Bromyard as Hereford.

As we drove towards Bromyard Downs, I recalled summer days when I'd fly kites up there with Dad. One year he made me a model aeroplane with a motor.

Parking was difficult in the town centre. Everyone and their rubber duck had the same idea; Christmas shopping as well as seeing the wonderful decorations and lights.

We eventually found a spot near the river. Kylie spotted someone pulling out, and we nipped in before anyone else could.

I donned my glasses. The dark frames matched Mark's. Mr and Mrs Clark

Kent sprang to mind.

It was one of those special sun-kissed December days. We were all grateful that we'd remembered our gloves. Mark insisted on wearing his reindeer jumper and Santa hat. I didn't mind. It was almost Christmas, and nice for Kylie.

All around there were the sounds of Christmas pop songs and carols; Wham, Noddy Holder and Wizzard vied with *Silent Night*. The Beach Boys sang *Frosty the Snowman* and, for the first time in years, I found myself singing along.

'Wow,' Kylie exclaimed as we turned into the pedestrianised main street.

All around there were sights, sounds and aromas to tempt and delight our senses. The distinctive odour of chestnuts roasting led me to buy a bag for us all to enjoy. Eating in public was inadvisable for me, though I could manage a nibble or two. Chewing was the problem.

'See, Aunty! A reindeer.' A life-sized animated beast nodded away in a window next to a multihued Christmas tree. His nose was blinking red. 'Rudolph. It's Ruldolph. Like on Mark's jumper,' she exclaimed, jumping up and down.

Mark took her hand. 'Shall we go and see Santa now, poppet?'

Santa's grotto was nestled in one of the larger stores. We'd go to Woolworths later for some Pick'n'Mix for Kylie. A group of carollers were a reminder that this season was about more than gifts and jolly red-garbed men.

'You always loved this time of year, Kimberly,' Mark commented.

'Shtill do. Not too cold, though.' I smiled behind my draped scarf. There were some glances but most people were too busy to stare at strangers.

As we rounded a corner near the toy department, Mark stopped suddenly.

'It appears we're not the only ones hoping to see Santa,' he exclaimed.

A queue of thirty or so children with attendant adults snaked around the barriers that had been set up. There were signs pointing to the North Pole, with busy elves organising the next youngsters to sit on Santa's knee. A lady with a camera, dressed in her own festive costume, was taking snaps of each child and their happy parents with the very convincing smiling man. We could hear his booming voice.

'Five pounds?' Mark said, seeing the price for the photo package. Small ones for grandparents and a beautifully framed one for Mummy and Daddy — all signed by Santa himself.

'I'll p . . . pay. It'll be my treat, Mark.'

'It's not that, Kimberly. It's the price. Don't suppose you could arrest this photographer for highway robbery?' He grinned in such a warm yet cheeky way.

I thought of the headlines in the Herald. *Mrs Claus arrested. Santa breaks in via police station chimney in failed escape attempt.*

We joined the line. The photographer was snapping a Polaroid before adjusting the professional camera mounted on its tripod. Probably for easy identification, writing clients' details on the back. I imagined she'd post the package of photos out in the next day or so. There would be hundreds to develop and print.

In the background, above Santa's comfy armchair, was a sign, *XMAS 1995*. A sleigh with presents completed the picturesque ensemble.

Absent-mindedly we shuffled forward, Kylie's tiny hand in mine. In the other she clasped her list of preferred presents. The top one was Teacher Barbie with her chalkboard and two students.

I wondered if the glasses this Barbie wore were something Kylie identified with. The Rathaways all wore specs.

Watching the wonder in the children's eyes was heart-warming. Up ahead, one mischievous boy was tugging at Santa's beard but to no avail. This Santa had a real one; the sign of a professional who took his role very seriously. The buzz of amazement surrounded us, even from apathetic parents who assumed they'd seen it all before. Every child was in wonderland. All apart from one.

My eyes focused on her — a gloomy young girl with a brunette pageboy hairstyle. She was dragging her feet with body language that screamed indifference, or a sleepiness unusual for this time of day. Her mother was hustling her along. She passed a lolly to the girl, encouraging her to lick it.

'Poor kid,' I whispered to Mark as they left the podium and Santa to leave the Grotto.

'Yeah. Little tyke isn't enjoying this at all. Even that lollipop's not helping.'

It was true. Her mother seemed unsympathetic to her daughter's unhappiness. I supposed all she wanted was a photograph of her darling with Santa to show off to family and friends.

She was almost up to us, going the other way.

'Get a move on, Susie.'

A balloon popped, making us jump. Not Susie. Her face was blank — yet

222

there was something familiar there. Then they were both gone, swallowed up in the throng of people.

Kylie tugged my hand. The queue was moving.

'Sorry, Mark. Whash did you shay?'

'Only that I felt sorry for that kid — '

'It can't b . . . be. I'll jush be a moment.'

Letting go of Kylie's hand, I pushed past the throngs of people, searching everywhere for the mother and Susie. What were they wearing? Dark coats, was the frustrating answer; eighty percent of the crowd were dressed in a similar way.

I'd lost them — and the longer I searched, the further they'd be moving away from me. Mentally, I kicked myself, returning to Mark and Kylie.

'What's up, Kimberly? Where did you charge off to?' Mark asked, sensing my agitation.

I plunged my hands into my pockets, searching. Finally, I found it, uncrunching it to stare at the cherubic faces on our missing-person poster. I'd stuffed it in there a few days earlier.

'Kimberly?'

'That girl — Sushie?' I passed the paper to Mark. 'I'm sure that was Crystal B . . . Bowen.'

11

'Crystal Bowen. Think you're mistaken, Kimberly. Crystal is blonde, and that girl . . .'

'Had her hair dyed. I can tell.'

If I were correct, she'd also had it cut. But one thing I understood for sure was her face. My own facial problems appeared to have highlighted my perceptions of others.

'If you're certain,' Mark concurred. 'We should contact someone. Your sergeant?'

'No. Not yet.' I'd thought about it already. 'Susie' and her mother could be anywhere right now and Worcester was a big place to search on a hunch. If I only had a picture of 'Susie' . . .

The Christmas photographer! She'd have one. But she was so busy and she was by herself. There was no way I could interrupt her and explain it all.

Flashing my warrant card while I was like this, wouldn't help much.

I turned my attention to the queue. It wasn't very long behind us. Why was that? Then I spied a sign and peered over to read it.

Santa has to feed his reindeer. He'll be back at eleven.

A comfort break for Santa, and there were only four families behind us. Yes. That would work.

As best I could, I explained my plan to talk to Mrs Claus when Santa had his well-earned time off. I'd wait around after Kylie and the others saw Santa then have a word with her.

Mark suggested he'd go off with his sister to look at the nearby toys then return when I could speak to the camera lady.

It seemed to take a long time but Kylie saw Santa at last, spent her time with him and then posed, with Mark, for the obligatory photos. As Mrs Claus snapped away, I stood by her side. She was quite matronly, a good

226

match to Mr Claus. The rosy make-up on her cheeks and white wig were ideal for a woman trying to make little ones feel at ease while their pictures were taken.

'Poor old Santa,' she commented in a chatty way. 'Prostate trouble. Needs the loo a lot.'

I didn't think she'd noticed my covered face. As she straightened up, she stepped back on witnessing my disguise. It was off-putting, though I understood her reaction.

I'd written a note, and showed it to her as she half-ignored me, tidying away spent rolls of film. The warrant card grabbed her attention more.

The note read, *I'm a detective investigating the abduction of two girls from Hereford. I think you just photographed one. May I see your Polaroids? About twelve from the end. Susie?*

Mrs Claus re-read my letter before examining me. 'Your face. You're that policewoman who almost drowned. DC

Winters or something. Yes, of course I'll help.'

She opened her box containing the Polaroids with addresses written on the back. Meanwhile, I flattened out the picture of Crystal and Scarlett to compare them.

Mark and Kylie came back to stand by my side. Good. I was reluctant to speak too much in this very public place. Already my covered face was drawing too much attention from passers-by.

'Is this the girl?'

She put the photo on the table by Santa's sleigh then shone a spotlight on it. Putting my picture next to it, I thought it was indeed Crystal. The blonde flouncy curls were gone, replaced by the chestnut short style. Yet it was clear that her eyebrows were still blonde and every other feature was the same as Crystal's.

The three of us stared intently at the comparison. Kylie watched us quietly.

'It's her, Kimberly. You were right.

You've found Crystal.' Mark clapped me on the shoulder.

Reaching to flip over the photograph, Mrs Claus put her hand on mine to stop me.

'What are you doing, Detective?'

Need name and address, I wrote, perplexed at her attitude. Along with the Polaroids plus film, we could go to HQ, have the photos printed to confirm it was Crystal, then go and get her. I was praying Scarlett would be imprisoned there also.

'Oh no, you don't. Client confidentiality. I can't let any Tom, Dick or Harriet abuse the trust that my customers place in my integrity. I have a reputation to maintain.'

Mrs Claus took the photo in her hand, then folded her arms across her ample bosom.

It was impossible to believe, yet that's what she was doing. As I was steeling myself to let fly with every insult I could slur, Mark stepped forward with his calming voice and boyish charm.

'Calm yourself, DC Frost. This lady is quite right to protect the identity of this kidnapper.'

'What — ?' I half said before he shushed me.

'After all,' he continued with a droll smile, 'Crystal's parents, the newspapers and TV stations will understand you're not intentionally protecting this criminal. And if this person spirits Crystal away again while you mess the police around, no one could possibly blame you.'

He half-turned to leave before adding, 'On the other hand, if we could announce that the owner of . . . ' he checked the signage, 'of Kute Kiddies Photographers was instrumental in discovering the whereabouts of these missing girls? I imagine the publicity would be . . . considerable.'

He began walking away, leading me and Kylie with him. It took scant seconds before Mrs Claus ran in front of us.

'Hold on, Detective. Let's not be

hasty. I didn't actually say you couldn't check the details.' She was quite agitated. I tried to grin under my scarf. Mark had achieved a sort of win-win situation.

It only took a few minutes to make the arrangements we needed. I'd take the Polaroid of Crystal, plus the roll of film with the professional photographs taken of Crystal, Kylie and quite a few others. The police would develop the film and print Crystal's photos from the negatives. Having taken great care to get it just right, the negatives would be returned to Mrs Claus tonight for her to do her own printing.

The three of us headed off towards Hereford Police HQ. Mark had rung DS Cameron, who was expecting me and the photos. He assured us they'd have the lab ready and agreed that we had a breakthrough on the case.

Kylie was good as gold about the interrupted day, but Mark had prom- ised her some special treats once we reached Hereford. We were only a few miles from Worcester and I was regretting the decision to drive to Hereford because of the horrendous traffic jams.

'Must be an accident ahead,' said Mark. 'Blue lights coming up behind us. I'll move over.'

The lights and sirens quickly came closer until a powerful police estate pulled alongside us. The second officer signalled Mark to pull over.

'Great. What was I doing wrong?' Mark moaned. 'I was hardly speeding.'

One of the officers stepped out after we had both pulled to the side of the road. Instead to going to Mark's side, he approached me.

'DC Frost. You're coming with us.'

What's going on? I wondered. Then he opened my door.

'We're to escort you to Hereford. DCI Aldershot's sent us. Bring the photos, please. We'll get you there much faster, Miss.'

I saw Kylie's eyes wide open at the excitement. Flashing blue lights, a police car and a real-life policeman in uniform.

'Room for one more?' I asked boldly.

'Don't see why not. You'd best hurry, though.'

It was a spur-of-the-moment decision but it felt right. Mark could meet us there.

'Would you like to go with Kimberly in that police car, Kylie?' Mark asked.

'Yes, please!' the seven-year-old squeaked. She had unbuckled her seat belt and was being help out by the burly officer before I knew it. This would be one special day for her.

★   ★   ★

Commandeering a police high-speed vehicle made sense. It was a shame that, even though we were both part of West Mercia Constabulary, there were still divisions between county forces. Yet it would make our journey much faster, and the address 'Susie's mother' gave was close to Hereford.

'Make sure your seat belts are good and tight, you two,' the younger of the two officers advised, glancing over his shoulder. 'We're going to be going very fast once we're through this traffic.'

The siren began again as we pulled out into the banked-up traffic. Like the Biblical Red Sea, cars parted to let us through. It was a big Volvo estate, a traffic car. Behind our bench seat were traffic cones and rescue equipment, as this car normally would patrol the M5.

'How fast?' I asked the driver over the siren.

'One hundred thirty on the motorways. Right now, we'll stay under a hundred, DC Frost. By the way, me and Terry here were very impressed with what you did to help with the missing girls. When we heard you had a lead and were heading up to Hereford, we asked to assist. Both of us have kids of our own, you see.'

We chatted as we picked up speed on the most direct route. Kylie sat entranced. It was quite possibly even more exciting than meeting Santa.

When we arrived at our destination, the officers kindly posed for a quick photo with their vehicle and Kylie for a souvenir. Then we hurried inside, where a WPC took charge of Kylie and a technician took the precious roll of film.

'Rush job?' she confirmed. 'Twenty minutes.'

Take care of the negatives, I wrote. *Lots of memories there.*

The Worcestershire offices would return the film negatives to Mrs Claus as promised before reporting back to their HQ at the former manor house of Hindlip Hall.

In the meantime, I showed the Polaroid photo from Santa's Grotto to Steven.

'It's hard to be certain if this Susie is actually Crystal, Kimberly. It's fuzzy. We can't raid this woman's home on a guess.'

I took out my almost full note pad.

That's why I brought the film. What

details do we have about the woman?

Steven showed me. He'd been busy in the time since I'd rung him.

'Heather Dukinfield. Forty-nine years old. Divorced. No children. We have her car reg make, model and colour. Lives in a big old detached Georgian place in the country. No convictions, but she was questioned years ago about stealing from a charity she was in charge of. School teacher, of all things. Now highly respected by her employer. Big church-goer. Bit like you.'

His prompt reminded me that I had been lax lately. Too many shifts on Sundays, too easy to make excuses. Maybe tomorrow I'd revisit my old church and priest in Bromyard.

'I had an unmarked car do a drive-by. No sign of her vehicle. Guess she's still out shopping — just like my missus. Buying everything under the sun — including new socks for yours truly, I've no doubt.' He had a little laugh.

*   *   *

We didn't have long to wait for the prints of the photos to be brought in. Mark had arrived minutes earlier, but was only staying long enough for a progress report before taking Kylie home. Steven told me I'd get a lift home with someone if this Susie was in fact Crystal. If not, I could go with Mark, having made a fool of myself chasing shadows.

Steven spread the montage of blown-up photos before us on the table in the briefing room.

'Hmm. I see what you mean, Kimberly. She does appear to be one spaced-out kid. No smile, blank, staring eyes. Mother seems normal enough — almost OTT excited, by the looks of her. And you said she gave the kid a lollipop? Could be coincidence, but I'm a copper. I don't believe in coincidences.'

He produced magnifying glasses for each of us to examine the prints in minute detail.

Steven commented first.

'Blonde eyebrows. Definitely. And the skin colour is wrong for a brunette.'

Mark pointed to some item on Susie's wrist.

'There's a bracelet on photo two with what resembles small dangly things. Can you make them out, anyone? My eyesight's not brilliant.'

'Looksh like a horse. And a fairy? Sharge?'

My sergeant was already flipping through details of what Crystal had been wearing when she was abducted.

'Bingo. Charm bracelet. Unicorn. Fairy and princess. Gold with a silver clasp and chain.'

'Can't shee shilver on thish one . . . but on number three, yesh.'

Detective Sergeant Cameron put down the magnifying glass and jumped to his feet.

'It's her. Dear Lord. You two have found Crystal. I can't believe it. And if we've located Crystal . . . ?'

'Scarlett too?' Mark interrupted.

238

'We can only pray. You're coming with me, Kimberly. You deserve to see this through. Plus, with you around, I feel I have my own lucky charm. There was talk of scaling down the op to find them, but now . . . Mr Rathaway? Are you coming? You're our technology expert after all. She might be this Lollipop Man's accomplice — the one who first contacted that Jessica home-help.'

Mark looked uncomfortable.

'I can't. My sister. It was supposed to be her special day out. Already she's spent ages here.'

'That's no problem. I happen to be expecting a rather lovely lady and her two teenage daughters, who'd love nothing better than to pamper a young girl with meals out and ice-creams and toys. They should be here any moment.'

I laughed without thinking and found myself wiping my mouth afterwards. 'Your f . . . family?'

'Guilty as charged, DC Frost. They drop in to see me here from time to time. Christmas cake for all the staff is a Mrs Cameron tradition.

'Also, I had a feeling that your hunch about this Susie being Crystal would be right. Heaven knows we needed a Christmas miracle to find them.'

★　★　★

Some time later, the three of us were sitting outside Heather Dukinfield's home. Another four police in civvies were waiting in another car. Once again, it was radio silence in case the police frequencies were being listened to.

'It's like déja vu all over again,' Mark said from the rear seat. I wondered if he were joking, or that he didn't have a clue what déja vu really meant.

He was right, though; here we were sitting in a car waiting to pounce on a suspected kidnapper and hoping to find the Bowen children. If Dad read it in one of his detective novels, I'm positive he'd moan about weak writing using the same scenario over and over again — even if this residence was at the opposite end of the scale to Guy's caravan.

Realistically this is what detectives do a lot. Watch and wait. Surveillance. Though I thought the term 'dying of boredom' was more appropriate.

'When can we go in?' Mark asked yet again. Honestly, it was as bad as when we used to go on holidays to Pontins with Mark tagging along. He'd constantly asked, 'Are we there yet?' Some things about my new boyfriend would never change. I wouldn't want it to be otherwise.

Steven's mobile phone rang.

'You have? . . . Well, about time. Meet me at the front door. Bring your torches. It's getting dark and perhaps she's stashed the children out there.' He disconnected the call. 'Right, you two. We have our search warrant. Time to go a-calling on Miss Dukinfield.'

Then Steven pointed at Mark's chest. 'Oh. And make sure that jumper of

241

yours is covered up. If we do arrest this Heather woman, I don't want her solicitor screaming for a mis-trial because you traumatised her.'

'It's only a reindeer jumper,' Mark began. 'And you haven't seen the best part.' He pressed something and the nose lit up.

'Super, eh? Rigged it up myself.'

Steven's eyes opened wide in shock.

'I don't care. It scares me even more now and I've seen all sorts of horrors. Cover it.'

Poor Mark. In trouble again.

* * *

Miss Dukinfield opened the door smiling. We had no idea who she may have been expecting, but Steven explaining who we were and demanding to search her house wasn't them. Reluctantly she let us all enter.

Her hall was indeed decked with boughs of holly. Christmas decorations and lights were everywhere. Heather

242

was obviously a Christmas person — although that's where the resemblance to my Mark ended.

'What are you hoping to find, Detective Sergeant?' she calmly enquired. She'd changed into jeans and a loose gold sparkly jumper, and was much more relaxed than the rather manic woman I'd seen earlier.

If she recognised me or wondered about my appearance, she didn't comment. If anything, she avoided eye contact.

'A missing child or two,' he replied, bluntly.

Miss Dukinfield stepped aside to allow our group to enter.

'You won't find anyone here but me, Sergeant.'

'We'll see. In the meantime, perhaps you can explain these photographs from earlier today.'

That shook her a little. I was content to watch her reactions and body language. It was what I did best. Whatever my sergeant did was designed to catch her out, knocking her off balance.

She glanced outside before closing the door on the freezing weather. We went into what she called her parlour. The bay windows were festooned with strings of Christmas lights, the curtains pulled aside so that her elaborate display was there for all to see from the busy road.

'That was my . . . niece. Susie.' She smiled. It was obvious she wasn't going to admit defeat, choosing to mess with us instead.

'The photographer and Santa heard you refer to yourself as her mother,' Steven countered.

'Obviously they misheard me, officer. The din in there was quite something. Wouldn't you agree, Detective Constable Kimberly Frost?'

I remained impassive. She was an intelligent woman, more so than most of the criminals I'd come across, especially on this case. Teachers and reasonably smart generally went together. She'd put two and two together as far as who'd seen her this morning and who I was.

'Let's get this right. You're adamant that the girl in these photos is your niece, Miss Dukinfield. I find that very strange. One might even suggest it was inexplicable or anomalous or even incredulous if one were so inclined.'

My superior was flexing his mental muscles with this woman, I could see. And it was working.

'Why?' I asked.

'Because Miss Heather Gwendolyn Dukinfield, born fifth of November 1949, doesn't have a niece. In fact, she doesn't have anyone. She's just a sad middle-aged spinster who likes to imagine that someone loves her.'

All Heather's pretence of being in control evaporated. She burst into tears, collapsing into the chintz-covered armchair behind her. Neither of us moved to help her. Somewhere in this vast house she had Crystal imprisoned and it was our team's job to find her.

Fifteen minutes passed . . . Twenty. Each team reported back without success. They'd found a bedroom with bolts on the outside. It was filled with children's clothing and toys for a girl, most of them covered with dust. They'd been there years.

'Check the grounds and outbuildings. She has to be here,' my boss said to the other officers.

Steven was becoming concerned and Miss Dukinfield had clammed up, insisting on her right to a solicitor. Nonetheless, she was hiding something. Her eyes darted to the front window whenever she thought we weren't watching her. I had excellent peripheral vision — at least in my right eye.

Mark entered. 'I've checked her computer.'

Heather looked up, seemingly puzzled.

'Yes, I do realise it was password protected, Miss Dukinfield. However, I have to tell you that your first name isn't a very clever password.' He addressed Steven. 'Lots of Yahoo mail between her and someone called Sweetie. No prizes for guessing who that is. All about 'adopting' a young girl because she's too much trouble. Even a photo. It's Crystal for certain — and there's an empty hair dye bottle, plus lots of blonde hair, in the wheelie bin.'

Steven knelt down in front of Heather.

'What do you have to say about that, lady? Where have you hidden Crystal Bowen?'

'I want my lawyer, Sergeant.' She stared at everywhere but the window.

He swore. 'It's useless. We'll take her down to the station. See if she comes clean with a solicitor there.'

I beckoned him aside. 'You don't think . . . '

'That she's dead and buried? No, Kimberly. This morning she was showing her 'daughter' off to the world. Pretty photos to put in frames. She's keeping her drugged, I reckon, and hopes Crystal will become her little child, to be dressed and fussed over. She's a sick lady, but she's no killer.'

Overhearing our conversation, Heather became very agitated. She was about to say something but decided against it. Instead she stood, holding her hands out for a female officer to cuff her. She peered through the glass. It was obviously freezing out there.

'Whash she intereshted in out there?' I asked. 'Theresh nothing . . . only the road.'

On impulse I walked to the window. Nothing but darkness and the orange glow of a street light a hundred yards or so down the sparsely lit road. Then a van went by and I saw it — a silhouette momentarily outlined by the van lights.

'Her car.'

'Can't be. We already searched it. It's in the garage,' an officer replied.

I spun around to confront Heather. There was panic in her eyes.

'Another car. Outshide . . . on the road.'

'No. You can't search it! It's not on

my property,' I heard her protest. Mark and I were already in the hall, throwing open the front door. Two officers were following.

A blast of frigid air struck us in the face. We'd left our coats inside.

'Bloody hell. It's freezing,' Mark shouted. I was a faster sprinter but I crashed into some garden object. Mark arrived first, pulling the door handle.

'It's locked,' he yelled. 'Torch. Quickly.' The four of us were there by now; Flashlights danced around the car interior as others headed our way from the illuminated house.

'Must be the boot.' His voice was frantic.

'Locked,' shouted a female constable from behind the car. We needed to break in.

'Baton?' I asked the officer nearest me. She gave it to me, having snapped it to its full size. The tactical baton could pack quite a punch.

'Stand back!' I swung the weapon

against the passenger window. It shattered. Using the baton to clean bits of glass from the edges, I reached through to open the door.

'Boot release is under the right-hand dash,' Mark called to me. 'Hurry, Kimberly.'

I was hurrying, frantically searching for the release. There. I grabbed it then yanked hard. The lever moved and I heard the boot pop open.

'She's here. She's here.' A lengthy pause. I waited impatiently by the driver's door. Everyone else was crowded around the boot, shining torches inside. There was no room for me.

Mark's commentary continued. I stopped breathing, silently praying that she was still alive.

'No pulse. I can't feel her pulse.'

'Try her carotid,' a policewoman prompted.

Then Mark again.

'Dear Lord. She's freezing. Get me a blanket.'

'She's . . . she's . . . ?' I couldn't say the word. We were too late. Heather Dukinfield had said nothing, knowing the girl was dying in the cold only yards from where we'd been searching.

'What sort of monst — '

'Wait. There's a pulse. Weak.' The relief in his voice was palpable. Quickly he bundled her tiny body into some blankets and was carefully but quickly steered towards the warmth of the house. Right now, it was her best hope. The open fire.

There was shouting all around; garbled frantic cries. I stood, paralysed in deep shock, not daring to move in case that one step might somehow hurt poor little Crystal even more than she had been.

It was my fault. I should have realised . . . I should have known. I stood there for Heaven knows how long, gazing at the house with people calling and running. Sirens coming. Ambulance this time. They had to save her . . . had to.

Finally, a figure emerged from the front door, a silhouette against the light. A circle of whiteness danced over the icy grass, stopping at my feet.

'Kimberly? Are you still out here?' Steven walked slowly towards me.

'I couldn't ... I couldn't ... ' I mumbled incoherently. 'Itsh my f ... fault. I just can't be in there ... can't do anything. Is she ... ?'

Steven held out his arms. I buried my head in his chest. I could hear the tears in his voice, his breath catching in between heaving great sobs.

'She's ... going to be OK, Kimberly. Crystal's going to be fine.'

Surges of joy flooded through me. She was safe after all. Then I stopped.

'Sergeant. Not enough. We might have shaved Crystal, but where'sh Scarlett?'

12

Steven led me in to see young Crystal. I stayed back from the dramatic scene. There she was, her eyes open, watching the paramedics busying themselves around her. A drip was attached. He left me there with Mark by my side.

'Has she shaid anything?' I asked Mark as we stood by the dining room door. He'd been holding my hand tenderly.

'Just 'Mummy' a couple of times. She's pretty weak. The drugs that cow gave her — probably Valium to calm her down — plus being stuck in that fridge of a car boot won't have helped.

'The doctor over there told me her vitals are stabilising, though. It was touch and go but we were lucky. Alanna, that policewoman over there — she was a nurse in the Army. She knew exactly what to do.'

'Where's St . . . DS Cameron?' I enquired, glancing around but not seeing my sergeant anywhere.

'He just left to question that evil woman at the station. I cannot believe she'd allow that child to die like that.'

'Just thinking of shaving her own shkin. Or not thinking at all. Maybe she thought she'd get bail, then come back and get rid of the body. Who knowsh? Clearly not like any teacher we had. Thank goodnesh.'

Mark faced me.

'Do you realise your speech is improving, Kimberly? You can pronounce 'b's.'

I had wondered about that. Things did seem different.

'Try frowning . . . now smiling . . . Yes. It's definitely getting better. Can you close your eyelid? No. Sadly not yet. But things are definitely happening.'

★ ★ ★

254

We were taken to the station at the same time as the ambulance drove off with Crystal. I couldn't deal with any more tonight. Besides, I was on sick leave, wasn't I?

Heather's computer was now being examined by tech guys at the station, forensics were sifting through Heather Dukinfield's life, and police were out there interviewing anyone she knew.

The Bowens were being driven to the hospital by our DCI, and as for Heather herself . . . Quite honestly I hoped she'd rot in prison for the rest of her days.

Steven came out quickly to see us. He was leading the interview team.

'She's a cold fish, that one. Something not right in her head. No sense of morality at all.' He shook his head.

'And what about Scarlett?' I asked him, just as Kylie was brought up to us. She looked tired but very happy. We were about to head back to Bromyard.

'Another dead end. This Lollipop Man is very secretive. Paranoid to keep things compartmentalised. Apparently, he and some woman decided to keep Scarlett, but to pass Crystal on to Heather — those contact magazines again. At least we have one of the girls back.'

'Itsh not enough, Sergeant.'

'I know, Kimberly. I know. You all go home and think about what we've achieved. There aren't that many good days in this job, but today has been one of them.'

* * *

The following morning, I was up early doing my new routine of facial exercises in front of the mirror. Was I any better? I didn't notice any change so I asked myself if Mark had simply been trying to boost my confidence.

In a way, I felt elated at finding Crystal. Whether you could explain it as luck or good police work didn't matter. She'd soon be back with her parents, safe from the machinations of that disgusting creature who was now behind bars.

'Hurry up, Kimberly. That is, if you're still going to church,' Dad shouted up the stairs. We'd have a late breakfast on our return.

I pulled on my beanie hat and gloves before shouting 'Coming, Daddykinsh.'

There was only one more Sunday before Christmas, and St Joseph's was packed. The choir were singing *O Come All Ye Faithful* as we took our places in the pews. I glanced around to check if Mark or his family were there. His parents were on the other side of the aisle. Kylie waved politely, as did they. No Mark, though.

Father Newman was taking mass today, it seemed. He'd known me since I was about Kylie's age. As he surveyed the congregation he noticed me, hiding between Mum and Dad.

I pretended to sing hymns and carols, conscious that my voice wasn't up to it. Once it came to the concluding remarks, however, our maverick priest chose to put me on the spot.

'I'm pleased to see some newcomers to today's mass as well as some . . . shall we say errant lambs returning to the flock. Little Kimberly Frost, for instance — although not so little now, eh, young lady?'

I cringed, trying to sink into the wooden bench. People were looking round, staring. Flipping great.

'For those who may not have read the papers this morning, Kimberly is a Detective Constable with our hard-working local police. I remember her from her younger days, always chattering in lessons at school and in church while I was up here, trying to be heard. It was a competition at times; me rabbiting on about boring stuff like devotion, caring for others and self-sacrifice while she chattered about Boy George, some man called Marilyn and that pop group, the Police, with her friends. Maybe there's some connection there, her becoming a police officer. In any case, it does appear that,

258

miraculously, she must have taken notice of what I was saying as well.'

I prayed for a hole to appear below me so that I might escape.

'Please get up, Kimberly. You're among friends in this place of the Lord.'

By this time, those around had realised who I was. They prompted me to stand with gentle prods and words. Reluctantly I did, keeping my head bowed so that my less-than-perfect face wasn't on show for the congregation to witness.

'Thank you, Kimberly. Kimberly here was instrumental in finding the young missing girl, Crystal Bowen. It was in the papers this morning. The other child is still unaccounted for and we can only pray that Scarlett is well and will also be found soon.'

I remained standing, decidedly ill-at-ease. What else could Father Newman mortify me with? I didn't have long to wait.

'Commendable though her achieve-ments have been in this distressing case of children being abducted, that's not the reason I'm asking Kimberly to be on show. Detective Constable Frost. Will you read for us all on this coming Christmas Day?'

I was shocked. He was aware of my problem. How could he do this?

'No. I won't,' was my firm yet quiet response.

'I thought you might say that, Kimberly. Is it because you are suffering from an affliction called Bell's Palsy that affects your facial muscles? Do you feel perhaps, self-conscious — different from the rest of us healthy, normal people?'

Blinking hell. This felt like an interrogation where I was being steered into a corner by an adept copper. Father Newman imagined himself as the investigative fictional cleric, Father Brown.

Hesitantly I replied. 'It . . . it might be, Father.'

'Please bear with me, ladies and gentlemen, boys and girls. And don't be afraid to join our youthful detective in standing as I share my thoughts with you. Kimberly feels alone. Is there anyone else here who has had Bell's Palsy? Please stand or, if you cannot, put your hand up.'

Slowly two women and a man rose to their feet. I recognised one as my former teacher, the one with the not-quite-right smile. That explained a lot.

'Thank you. Please remain standing. Now, which of you out there have had a stroke?'

This time over a dozen rose or held up a hand.

'Looks like a few of us aren't quite one hundred percent perfect. Now those of you with heart conditions. Please join us.'

This time the good Father held his own arm aloft. That was a shock to me, though I had heard rumours. By this time, I was upright and not as ashamed to show my temporary disfigurement.

And so it went on. Arthritis, kidney

problems and many other health problems. In the end Father Newman asked if there were any conditions he'd not mentioned. A few more joined the rest of us, calling out their affliction almost proudly.

'Thank you all,' he said. 'You may all sit now. Not that these old pews are all that comfortable.' I moved to sit down once more.

'Not you, young Kimberly. Not yet.' He took a deep breath. 'Everyone who has joined Kimberly has bared their own souls today. I suspect that many of you have not shared your own health ailments so publicly before. I know I haven't.' There were the sound of muted laughter.

'We are all far from perfect. In some cases, our illness may be lifelong, life-changing or life-limiting. Some may have problems easily visible to others whereas others may appear 'normal' yet be suffering within. We should all remember though, that it is the feelings in our hearts that define us as people.'

He paused, directing his penetrating gaze again in my direction.

'I ask you again, Detective Constable Kimberly Frost. Will you accept my invitation to read for us all this Christmas Day?'

Father Newman had made his point. It had been a chastening yet uplifting few minutes.

'I acchept with gratitude, Father.'

Outside the church, the weather was relatively warm though the skies were clear. Father Newman came to speak to me, along with my parents.

'I trust it wasn't too traumatic, Kimberly. Nothing compared to having a weapon pointed at you or almost drowning.'

'Shome warning might have helped, Father,' I conceded. 'Thish problem of mine ish hard enough without being p . . . put under a spotlight.'

'You did well, my child. And you should be grateful I never mentioned you smoking behind the presbytery that time.'

Dad glared at me. I shrugged. It had been just the once. The priest continued.

'I had expected to see young Mark here with you today. Your boyfriend, I hear. About time.'

I was surprised. 'Wash it that obvious?'

'Back in school? Yes. To everyone bar your good self, it seems. I wish you both years of happiness — and before you ask, it would be my pleasure to join you together in holy matrimony.' He gave me a wink.

'Flipping heck! Give ush a break, Father. Itsh only been a few daysh.'

'Destiny is inevitable, Kimberly. But you know what feels right. Don't you?'

I smiled feebly. 'No preshure then, Father.'

★ ★ ★

Lunch was actually a late breakfast but it was the full-on English one. When I asked to finish it off with a mince pie and cream, Mum threw her hands up in the air.

'The girl's got a cast-iron stomach,' she said, and left Dad and me to clean up later.

Dad nudged me.

'I just might join you with that dessert, Kimberly. After all, it is almost Christmas. Wouldn't want those mince pies to go off now, would we?'

Later, I rang the hospital to check on Crystal's progress. Well, Mum rang on my behalf. Telephone conversations were exasperating for me.

'Information for family only, they're saying. There's been a lot of reporters.'

Then I recalled Steven saying he'd arranged a code word for me when he'd rung last night.

'Tell them, *Wonder Woman*.'

Mum did so, listened then put the phone down.

'She's recovering well. It was just the cold . . . and those drugs that bitch gave her.'

Mother. You ushed the 'b' word!' I admonished.

'Remember when I told you there are times when swearing is all right? This is one of those times. I cannot imagine any woman hurting a child like that.'

To be fair, Crystal had been fed well and was clean and well dressed. She'd told the nurses that Heather had brushed her hair a lot, almost treating her like a baby doll in her perfect imaginary world.

Mark arrived around three. He'd been at headquarters again. Not surprisingly, he'd been offered a full-time job there in a consultancy role. His ideas and computing skills were being recognised as the way to lead our division into the twenty-first century.

'Any nearer finding Scarlett?' I asked.

'Unfortunately, not. This Lollipop Man is very adept at covering his tracks. I doubt we'll spot *her* visiting Father Christmas this year. He's not that stupid.'

I began to sob, realising he was

probably correct.

'They're keeping Crystal in hospital until Wednesday. Her parents have been there all the time with a policewoman keeping watch. You wouldn't believe how grateful they are. They've invited us both over on Wednesday afternoon.'

Then he remembered another thing to mention.

'Heard about church this morning from Dad,' he commented in a matter-of-fact way. 'Glad I wasn't there for Father Newman to pick on me too. Still, I would have loved to see it. Pity no one had a video camera.'

'Yesh. Not my finesht moment. Father had a word later about ush. Talking about marriage already.'

His eyes lit up. 'And?'

'Look, Mark. You might have alwaysh loved me but a week ago, I wash sthill in love with Barry. I can't change that quickly. I want there to be an ush, but I'll need shome time. You undershtand?'

'Of course. Perhaps a sort of kiss will

267

keep me interested, Kimberly. You don't want me finding someone else, do you? Like that Alanna constable we met last night?'

'You're joking, aren't you?' I knew he was, though a kiss would help keep him interested . . . plus it would help me too . . . a lot.

Mum entered just as we were into a full-on embrace. She excused herself, murmuring about mince pies being some sort of aphrodisiac and that she'd better hide them from Dad.

Mark then suggested that I join him and Kylie at the *Cinderella* panto being held down the road at the Conquest Theatre. That resulted in a lot of pantomime jokes, to-ing and fro-ing with 'It's behind you' and 'Oh no, he didn't.' The odd cushion may have been thrown.

Dad then came in, searching for the mince pies.

'We've set the Trivial Pursuit board up, you two. Found it in the loft. How about a game together like the old days?

Guys versus girls?'

We agreed and put the cushions back before joining them in the dining room.

'Hope you remember your sport trivia, Mark,' Dad said.

'No problems, Ted.' Mark gave me a sly wink. When it came to sport my Mark didn't have a clue. It was going to be a whitewash . . . Girl power for sure. My Wonder Woman bracelets were already empowering me.

* * *

The pantomime was predictable, very noisy and lots of fun. It was exactly what I needed. Kylie had a great time, too.

Monday and Tuesday passed quickly. I had my physio appointment on the Monday. This time Mum drove me into Hereford. She explained there were some extra presents that needed buying.

During my treatment, the nurses commented that I was showing signs of improvement. They agreed it was unusual this early on. It had been a little over a week since I'd been struck down.

What a week it had been, too; almost drowning, losing one boyfriend, gaining another, tracking down a guy demanding a ransom, finding Crystal and arresting the woman who'd been passing her off as her own. Mark was the best part, but finding Crystal was best too in a different way.

I took Kylie swimming on Tuesday after Mum and I arrived back in Bromyard, then Mark came around for tea with us all. It was his treat. Fish and chips, though not as good as Mrs Wu's. Eating was gradually becoming less messy. It was good to feel I was improving.

For some reason, the conversation drifted round to Kylie's last birthday party in mid-November. I'd been on duty that day so wasn't there. Thinking about it, Mark's and Kylie's lives had often been interwoven with my parents and mine.

'Did you have a good time, Kylie?' Mum asked.

'Yes, Aunty Linda. It was magical,' Kylie replied before bursting into a fit of giggles.

'Magical, sweetheart?' Mum said, as she cut up her piece of cod. 'What do you mean?'

Mark explained. 'There was a magician there. My gift. He was very good, too.'

'Yes. He made things disappear with his wand. Abrykadabry. Poof. And the bunny rabbit vanished like she was unvisible. Then he brought her back again from his tall black hat.'

Dad made a comment under his breath.

'Aunty Linda must be a magician too. She made the three hundred pounds I gave her today vanish as well. Poof. Just like that.'

We burst out laughing. Mum pinched his cheek.

'Essential presents for everyone, Ted. I even bought you some. I'll give you a clue. They go on those smelly feet of yours.'

The same as Steven's gifts at Christmas, I remembered. It seemed to be what all married men were given. Mum held her nose. That brought more laughter.

It was only later, when Mark had taken Kylie home, that the three of us retired to our comfy lounge. We each had a glass of some Australian red wine, mine in the training mug.

'That Kylie is a lovely girl. Reminds me of you at that age, kitten. What she said about invisibility and making objects disappear, has me thinking about you-know-who.'

Yeah. That blinking Lollipop Man.

'You said from the shtart that he wash into divershions and you were right. I wish he'd dishappear for good.'

'There are two types of invisibility, kitten. Remember Wonder Woman's plane in the comics and that telly show? The one she kept bumping her head on because she couldn't see it?'

'Yeah. It ushed to be a magical horse, I think, then it changed.'

Dad sat back in his chair.

'That's exactly it, Kimberly. The second type of invisibility. To be hiding in plain sight, disguised as something or someone different.'

Mum decided to join in.

'Like Clark Kent wearing glasses so that people don't know he's Batman?'

Dad and I grinned. Mum never could understand comics and superheroes.

'Oh . . . Clark Kent is Superman, isn't he? I forgot. But I see where you're both going. Tell me what you actually know about this Lollipop Man of yours.'

I thought about our evidence.

'Well. He'sh a man — '

Mum was ready with her telling response.

'Is he?'

I stared at her in complete surprise. Out of the mouths of babes and intuitive mothers. A kiss for that brilliance was definitely in order.

13

Dad wasn't following our train of thought. He stared at us blankly. Poor Dad. It must have been so frustrating to be born a man.

Mum continued. 'What if 'he's' a she? Calling herself a man is the ultimate lie. No self-respecting woman would stoop so low; no offence, Ted.'

At last, he nodded his head in understanding.

'None taken, darling. Us men are single-minded thinkers. This is so outlandish yet it makes perfect sense. This fixation on taking a child to keep and giving the other girl, Crystal, to a woman who loved to play with dolls. This whole abduction thing is about motherhood.'

It was. Why couldn't I have seen it earlier? All those clues from the Bowens' house. I stood up to retrieve the file I'd been sifting through.

'Mum. Can you p . . . please write theshe pointsh down. Here's my notebook.'

'One. Shoes.' The impressions from the kidnappers' shoes were large inside, but there were size six ones in the mud outside the laundry window. What if Lollipop Woman put on larger shoes to confuse us?

'Two. The beds being neatly arranged.'

Up until now it made no sense. Was it habit, or simply to delay the thought that there was anything amiss? Mrs Bowen had told us that Crystal enjoyed doing it, yet she couldn't have done on the night of the abduction. She'd been knocked out with chloroform.

'Three . . . No idea.'

I couldn't think straight. My eye was really hurting. Time for some drops. Dad helped me, using the dropper as I tipped my head backwards.

'Three,' Mum offered. 'All the sightings were of a woman.'

Hmm. She'd been a naughty mummy, reading the confidential files, it appeared.

She was right, though. The police had assumed the woman who had been involved was an accomplice. Yet it made sense for her to be the one in control, making certain that her plans were followed exactly.

In addition, Steven had told me Crystal had mentioned a 'nice lady' who fed her and Scarlett.

I nodded for her to record it on the page.

Everything was making sense now. Our enquiries and questions had all been based on a false premise . . . that the mastermind behind the abduction was male.

Between us, we refined the information then Dad phoned Steven to suggest what we'd deduced. We waited expectantly. When Dad hung up, he gave us a thumbs-up sign. Steven would get the team to review everything, including revisiting the Bowens. We'd asked about men with grudges . . . never women.

⋆   ⋆   ⋆

Wednesday; the twentieth of December. It was time to visit the Bowens to find out how Crystal was doing.

Mark, Steven and I arrived around two. I'd had an early session with the magnetometer at the hospital. This time of the day was generally better for speaking, as the muscles that were working became more sluggish at night.

We'd met up at the station, where there was a renewed drive to find our mysterious mastermind. All the prisoners had been interviewed again, as had those who'd had any connection to the messages that had been sent.

Meeting Crystal properly for the first time was going to be emotional. There was a loving embrace for Mark and me from the Bowens before we were led through to their spacious lounge. Drinks and nibbles were served while we settled down to address the most important issues.

'Crystal went for a sleep earlier. I'll see if she's awake. She doesn't remember much from the week she was gone; a blessing, I think. Either the drugs she was given or her way of dealing with it.'

Candice left us with her husband, Daniel.

'Has she has any nightmares? Flashbacks?' Steven asked him.

'A bit. It's early days. She'll be seen by a trauma counsellor when the doctors think she's ready. It would seem that she was very brave, trying to protect little Scarlett as much as she could. Part of the reason the kidnapper passed her on to this Dukinfield woman. Lots of screaming and fighting. We believe Crystal made herself too much trouble, especially together with Scarlett.'

Crystal was led in by her mum, appearing much brighter than when I'd last seen her. There was an unnatural timidity though. I couldn't blame her for that, considering what she had been through.

'Crystal. These are the people who helped rescue you. Their names are Kimberly and Mark.'

Crystal had come closer of her own free will, then hugged Mark. The reindeer on his jumper immediately caught her childish attention.

'Reindeer,' she said. 'Red nose — like you.'

'My nose isn't red, is it?' He rubbed it, making it redder. Crystal giggled.

'Thank you, Mr Mark,' she said before stepping back to examine my face. She reached out to touch my left cheek. I didn't budge. At last, her little arms encompassed me.

'You saved me, Kimberly. Did a bad lady hurt you, too?'

'Hurt?' I asked, wondering if this lovely girl had been injured.

Daniel shook his head.

'No injuries. It's just her way of saying what occurred.' That was a relief.

'No, Crystal. It's just a little problem

with my face. It's getting better.'

That seemed to satisfy her and she settled down between us on the large settee. It was then she noticed my heavy bracelets poking out from my sleeves, and briefly twirled them round.

I half listened to Steven talking to her parents while also chatting to Crystal.

Eventually, her attention turned to Mark and his glasses. I was glad. He was much better with children, I'd realised over the years. Suddenly he reached down the neck of his V-necked jumper. Rudolph's nose began glowing. Everyone ceased their conversations to stare.

'That stupid pullover.' Steven pointed, tongue-in-cheek. 'Don't you have any other clothes to wear, Rathaway?'

Mark feigned offence. 'Of course I do. I have one with a fox, one with a tiger and two with dinosaurs. But I can only wear Rudy here at Christmas, can't I? How daft do you think I am?'

I suspected Steven was ready to answer that so I jumped in rapidly.

'Mark's mother likes to knit. And I think he looks very fetching wearing them.'

Steven grinned. 'You two are as dippy as each other, though I have to admit, you're a great team. But tell us, Mr Rathaway. Why is old Rudy's nose so bright all of a sudden? Any stronger and I'll need my sunglasses.'

'I've connected a much more powerful battery. Gets all the girls' attention — though I'm happy just to have Kimberly's.'

'Very diplomatic,' I commented, feeling a tinge of jealousy.

Steven brought us back to the reason we were here.

'Mr and Mrs Bowen. We need to talk without Miss Muffett overhearing.'

Candice stood up.

'Come on, Crystal. Let's go to your room. I bet Teddy Ruxpin wants to tell you a story. He's missed you a lot.'

Crystal clapped her hands. We all

knew how endearing the talking bear was. His mouth moved in time to the story cassettes you could buy to play inside his furry body. His arms and head moved too. Although he'd been around for years, young kids loved him and watching his cute nose and eyes moving, you could even imagine he was real.

Candice returned to sit down on a velvet settee near the telly. Steven was in an armchair.

'OK. What new discoveries have you made? Having Crystal back home is fantastic, but . . . ' Candice began before breaking down in tears. Her husband held her tightly. She recovered enough to apologise although she didn't need to.

'It's more of an idea that Kimberly came up with, along with her parents. I know it might sound crazy but we're now considering that Lollipop Man might be a woman.'

Candice leaned forward in her chair, elbows on her knees.

'Not so far-fetched, Detective Sergeant. Especially hearing what Crystal has mentioned since you people rescued her.'

This time it was her husband who spoke up.

'The trouble is, we've racked our brains. I'm a businessman but, as far as I'm aware, we have no enemies.'

It was a setback. We all sat quietly for a moment, the silence broken by the appearance of a very upset Crystal wiping her eyes.

Candice rushed to her.

'Honey. Whatever is the matter?'

'Teddy's not right. He's broked.'

'We can put new batteries in, Crystal. You know that,' her daddy suggested, kneeling in front of her.

'It's not that, Daddy. He talks but he's forgotted my name.'

Instantly we were all on guard.

Before we could ask, Mr Bowen explained. 'We had special tapes made so that Teddy's personalised. He says Crystal's name when he talks to her. We have other tapes for Scarlett too.'

Mark and Steven had the answer in a second. 'Someone's switched Teddy.'

'Why?' I asked. Then I answered my own question. 'Oh . . . To spy on us.'

We'd found our mole; not a police person passing on our secrets at all. This teddy was like me having a microphone on my body at the ransom drop off.

'Well. I'll be d . . . ' Steven began before I shushed him, nodding towards Crystal.

Mark interjected.

'Guess what, Crystal. I'm a special doctor for bears. Suppose I have a have a check on this teddy. Is that OK?'

She shrugged her tiny shoulders, fingering her now short hair. ''Spose. Maybe a chocolate marshmallow will make him better?'

Candice nodded. 'That's a very clever idea, honey. Why don't we find one for Teddy in the biscuit jar? And maybe one for you too?'

* * *

A few minutes after, Mark took the marshmallow to Teddy Ruxpin. He returned holding a small device and batteries in his hand.

'Is that . . . ?' Candice exclaimed before her husband clamped his hand over her mouth.

'It's a powerful radio, but don't worry. I've disconnected it. The batteries are probably dead anyway. It was secreted in the teddy. I'm guessing the abductors swapped them over on the night the girls were taken, and he or she listened to everything that happened in that bedroom. Talk about sneaky. Clever, too. This Lollipop individual is pretty knowledgeable about computers and electronics. Still ringing no bells?'

The two parents shook their heads.

'Could we trace the radio signal, like tracing a phone? No. Stupid question,' Candice said. 'Rhonda already told me you couldn't.'

I almost missed it.

'Rhonda? Your friend w . . . who came to shtay just after the girls dishappeared?'

'Yes. She was a godsend, Kimberly. I don't know how I could have coped without her visits.'

A thought was beginning to form in the back of my mind. Surely not. I'd met her — here. Could anybody be that brazen?

'Can you tell me about her, pleashe? A school fr . . . friend?'

Candice was getting a little annoyed. The quizzical expression on her face was altering.

'Kimberly. I really can't imagine how this can possibly help you, or this case.'

Steven glanced at both of us.

'Humour us, please, Mrs Bowen. It is important. I trust Kimberly's instincts implicitly. Given what she's achieved already in this case, you should too.'

Candice paused before lifting Crystal onto her knee. The young girl was more interested in staring at Mark's flashing jumper than taking any notice of what was being said.

'Of course. OK. Rhonda wasn't really a friend at school. In fact, we didn't get on because I think she resented me. She was brighter yet the boys preferred me. Rhonda was a little . . . abrasive when things didn't go her way. That's why I was surprised that she offered to stay with me. Other friends suggested I go to their places but I couldn't leave here. That's why I said OK when she offered to sleep here.'

'Thought she had her own family?'

By now both Mark and Steven were following my reasoning, bizarre though it was.

'Yes. A daughter about Scarlett's age. Her partner was caring for the girl while Rhonda stayed here. She'd phone him quite often, always asking about her 'precious treasure' as she called her.'

Candice turned to her own husband then back to us. 'You . . . you think . . . no. She couldn't be the one who took my girls. Why would she? She has her own girl.'

'Did you ever see this other girl, Mrs Bowen?' Steven inquired.

'A photo in her purse. That's all. In fact . . . she was the spitting image of Scarlett.'

14

Mark and Steven spent the next twenty minutes on their phones, each giving orders or suggestions to find out as much as they could about this Rhonda woman.

Candice didn't have a phone number for her. It was always Rhonda who'd rung to check on the latest update, or to offer to come over to help comfort the grieving mother. What began as a suspicion escalated with each new inquiry.

Mark's colleagues in the IT department at HQ were using computers to sift through vast amounts of information on electoral rolls, utility companies, library card registers, DVLA and so on. The discoveries that were gleaned from other electronic data banks were collated and faxed to us at the Bowens'.

There were false trails everywhere; aliases and so on, though the trail was narrowing as Rhonda's life was quickly unravelled. She'd previously been arrested as well as sectioned. One of the doctors who had treated her described her as having a chameleon personality capable of blending in to whatever role her mind would choose.

She did have a daughter — yet that daughter had passed away five weeks earlier.

Making enquiries at the address Candice had been given proved to be another dead end. This woman and her partner had woven multiple webs to confuse any person searching for her.

Yet another fax came through to Daniel's office. He was with Mark in there.

Meanwhile I was again comforting Candice. A WPC was caring for Crystal, because Candice was finding her misplaced trust in Rhonda difficult to process.

To be fair, this Rhonda was a master

liar and manipulator, as well as being skilled in hacking into computer networks. She'd done it before, crashing our police systems. A week or so ago, I'd never heard these strange terms like hacking, modems and floppy discs.

But Mark was right. These unusual-looking screens and keyboards were the future. The amount of personal details his team had unearthed about Rhonda would have taken me weeks on the phone and searching paper databanks. Even microfiche records were becoming obsolete.

Steven, Mark and Mr Bowen entered the room, Steven waving a sheaf of faxes.

'Gotcha, you little cow. Sorry, shouldn't use words like that.'

Candice stood up to join them.

'I've called her much worse, Detective Sergeant.' She had, too. And no wonder. She'd been betrayed in the most devious way possible.

Steven filled us in.

'We have armed officers on the way.

Turned out some elderly woman reported seeing Scarlett yesterday at this address. And before you ask, we've had over six hundred sightings to investigate, one by one.'

That explained the delay in checking.

Steven continued speaking.

'Since we have a name and description and addresses, our computers can sort through information much faster than people can. They matched one of Rhonda's aliases to the same address. When I just phoned this lady who reported the sighting, she told me that a blonde we think is Rhonda had just gone out. Happily, she'd seen a man and the little girl in the house not ten minutes ago.'

A second child being rescued from a woman holding them against their will was too much for me to deal with directly. Besides, DCI Aldershot was in charge of the raid on the council house outside Hereford. He wouldn't be waiting for us. This time it was imperative to retrieve Scarlett safe and sound without any further delay.

An undercover WPC had called at the pensioner's home, across the street from Rhonda's hiding place. She'd pretended to be a nurse in uniform in case Rhonda's partner was keeping watch. The officer had then phoned to report that she had indeed spied a girl in an upstairs window who matched Scarlett's description.

Once more, the police were in radio silence. If anyone had a police scanner, it would be Lollipop Lady and her partner.

We remained in the Bowens' lounge. The men were pacing impatiently as though walking would bring the news from the operation faster. I decided to take Candice to a place of safety — to her daughters' bedroom.

Crystal was there with the WPC. Immediately Crystal called her over to the colouring desk by the large window.

'Look, Mummy. I done a pretty drawing of a princess and a castle.'

My ploy could have gone either way,

but immediately Candice clicked into her mother mode, praising her child's colourful efforts then chatting to her. Underneath I could sense her apprehensions about the operation, yet she had suppressed them — at least for a little while.

When the three men joined us, there was joy in their eyes. Daniel spoke first.

'She's all right, love. Our Scarlett. They've found her.'

Candice rushed into his arms, burying her head in his chest. Crystal joined them.

Steven took Mark and me outside. His own eyes were misting.

'We just heard. DCI Aldershot phoned. The man's in custody and Scarlett's fine, physically at least. She's on her way to County Hospital and the guy, someone called Mike Wilkes, is in custody and heading for a cell at HQ.'

'Rhonda?'

'No sign, Kimberly. They could have waited, caught her as well but, on balance, they did the right thing.

Having two targets on the loose in that house with Scarlett could have been more difficult to manage. As it was, those new thermal imaging cameras allowed our team to move in and arrest him before he had any idea we were there. He was eating ice cream while watching the footie. Now we're aware of who and what Rhonda is, her days of freedom are most definitely numbered.'

It was almost an anticlimax. Our task of saving the girls who'd been taken from here almost thirteen days ago was done. The roller-coaster of my own health and emotions paled to nothing compared to that.

'What now?' Mark inquired.

'They'd like you to help process the house. It's less than two miles from Headquarters. Can't believe her arrogance, doing what she did, right under our noses. There is a police scanner as you suspected, plus a number of computers.

'You take your car, Mark. Kimberly

and I will go and talk to this Mike Wilkes and our WPC can take the Bowens to be reunited with Scarlett.'

We all left together, each heading for our own destination. It was already dark; the winter solstice, the shortest day. I pulled my overcoat tight around me. The dew-kissed grass was already turning icy white under the security lights that illuminated the driveway.

'Shee you later,' I told Mark with a quick kiss to remind him how much I thought of him. But those glasses of his had to go, pronto; replaced with something less nerdy, for sure.

*   *   *

The station was alive with the elation of rescuing Scarlett. Reporters had already gathered outside awaiting an official update from our chief and, I imagined, other reporters would be converging on the hospital.

DCI Aldershot called Steven in for the first interview with this Wilkes person. They were awaiting the duty solicitor.

Personally, I was bushed. It had been a mentally draining day for me and, even though the palsy wasn't that debilitating, I was aware I couldn't sit around here any longer.

I rang my parents to share the fantastic news and thank them for suggesting that breakthrough about the true sex of Lollipop. Somehow, I managed to speak clearly enough for them to understand.

'Where's Mark at the moment?' Mum asked.

'Procheshing the crime shene. He should be finished shoon . . . Hold on, Mum. Shomething's going on. I'll shee you in about half an hour.'

There was indeed a bit of a fuss.

'Whash happening?' I asked a uniformed sergeant heading to the car park.

'Kimberly? They've spotted that Rhonda on the main street of Hay-on-Wye. On foot. We're sending everyone over there. No way is she getting away.'

Great, I thought, wondering again if I should go as well. Realistically there was nothing I could do that the other officers couldn't. Within minutes, the bustling station was eerily quiet.

I decided that I could at least listen in down at the Communications room.

'Hi, Kimberly. How's it going, being a detective?' one of my colleagues said from behind a console. Clearly not everyone was aware of my affliction. The lights were subdued. There were two other officers manning their stations, phones close by.

'I'm on the shick,' I explained. 'Who called in the shighting?'

The young officer checked the computer screens in front of time, paging up to earlier.

'WPC 4537.'

'Are you sure, John? Thash my old number.'

They would never reassign a badge number that rapidly. It took only seconds for us to realise we'd been distracted yet again.

'John. Get onto the commanding officer. Quick.'

Not only had Rhonda used a police radio to send us miles away, but she'd pretended to be me.

Even as John desperately called everyone back, I asked myself, *What is Rhonda's game this time?*

15

'What could she possibly hope to achieve by sending us off to Hay?' Steven asked me on the radio. The mad pursuit had been cancelled and disgruntled officers were returning to their assigned duties.

I adjusted the headphones with attached microphone that John had passed to me. He sat in his swivel chair waiting for me to pass the headset back to him.

'No idea. To show us she'sh still in charge? Playing gamesh? Who knowsh?'

'Anyway, Kimberly. You get yourself home and make certain you thank those lovely parents of yours. We were all too close to the case. Couldn't see the wood for the trees, so to speak. The main thing is that the girls are both safe and Mrs Lollipop's luck won't last forever.'

'OK, Sharge. Keep me in the loop, pleashe.'

* * *

There was nothing to do but grab my little car and head back to Bromyard. The commuting was getting me down. Maybe I'd give Ludavine a ring and see about possibly renting again.

Then again, maybe not. I had a great feeling about me and Mark. Would moving in together make more sense — even though it was technically early days in our new, loving relationship? It was funny. I'd never considered doing that with my other boyfriends; not even that slimy slug, Barry. With Mark? It made perfect sense.

I'd seen a different side of my best friend since he'd declared his love for me. It had always been there; I'd simply chosen to ignore it. He was great with children, possibly from not entirely growing up himself. Being in love with the world's biggest kid. Why not? After all, Peter Pan and Wendy had a somewhat unconventional relationship too.

I hung around the radio room until it became evident that nothing major was going to happen. I'd seen *Assault On Precinct 13* years ago and half-wondered if Rhonda might storm the station single-handed once most of our officers were off chasing wild geese. I mean, she was prone to anything.

I tapped John on the shoulder. He turned and moved the headset slightly.

'I'm off. Headed home.'

'Take care, Kimberly. See you when-ever.'

★ ★ ★

The drive was uneventful apart from two idiots who didn't dip their high-beams when they should have. Our cul-de-sac was very festive when I drove in. I was glad to be home. Before I'd closed my driver's door, I heard someone running towards me, their heels click-clacking on the frosty path. A woman called out. I tensed a little.

'Kimberly. It's me. Danni.'

I relaxed. Danni was one of my fellow PCs from Hereford. 'Whatcha want, Danni?'

'Damn, it's cold,' she said, flapping her arms around her body. 'Come back to our car. It's important . . . and slightly warmer.'

She indicated a nondescript silhouette of a sedan at the entrance to our quiet street and was off before I could say anything.

At the car, I slipped into the back seat. The interior lamps came on again, Danni having already sat down up front. Her companion was one of the Sergeants, Bill something or other. He'd just transferred in.

'What's with your phone, Kimberly? DS Cameron's been trying to call.' Danni was agitated and I could hear her chattering teeth. She had gloves on, plus a blanket. They must have been here a while.

Checking my bag, I groaned. 'Dead battery.'

'That boyfriend of yours, the computer guy. He's disappeared. They reckon that lady kidnapper took him while — '

'While everyone wash heading to Wye.'

Bill explained that there had only been one forensics man and Mark in the home where they'd found Scarlett. The rest were chasing a very deceptive shadow around Herefordshire. That neighbour who'd noticed Scarlett at the window, reported seeing Rhonda pushing a man with glasses into an old car, then driving off.

The forensics guy was injured, but not seriously. I was grateful for that. So far no one had been killed, despite her threats especially to me.

'Where are they, then?' I was frantic, fearing the worst. Had Rhonda returned to her home wanting to retrieve things left there, or had she spied Mark's car and realised he was inside? I was positive my colleagues would be searching for Mark's car and its two occupants. I wanted to do something to help but was aware that, just like the Bowens, it was best to trust others.

'Thanksh for telling me.' It was then I understood that Steven could simply have rung my parents rather than dispatching a police car.

'You're here to watch out for me, aren't you?'

'The big bosses thought it was a sensible precaution, yes.' Danni was quite blunt. 'We've been here a while. Nothing suspicious except some woman opposite you, peeking through the curtains and some old bloke who was a bit under the weather. We'll stay here.'

'Come inshide in the warm. My parents wouldn't mind.'

Danni and Bill exchanged glances.

'No, we'd best stay here.'

'Appreciate it if you could bring us a hot Thermos, though. And some

Christmas cake if you have any.' Bill had been very aloof up till now but he was clearly suffering from the chilly weather too. Danni punched him playfully in the ribs. He added 'Please' at that point.

'No pr . . . probsh.' I opened the back door.

Danni stopped me with a gloved hand.

'Here, Kimberly. Take this radio. Just in case.'

She passed me her own. I made the short walk back praying that Mark would be OK. If I let myself break down outside, I'd never get as far as the house, so I walked mechanically, one step after another.

Using my key to open the front door, I called out, 'Mum, Dad, I'm home,' before hanging my coat, hat and gloves on the hooks by the hall door. I put the radio on the nearby table.

No response. I checked in the lounge and dining rooms. The lights were on and there was a smell of cooked food.

Something wasn't right.

'Mum? Where are you?'

'Your mum and dad are busy, Kim . . . ber . . . ly.' A female voice was coming from the kitchen. I edged towards there, pushing the door ajar.

'*Come in, come in, said the spider to the fly*, Kim . . . ber . . . ly,' she half sang in a slow, taunting voice. 'Come in and meet your maker, silly girl.'

I pushed the door completely open. Rhonda was leaning nonchalantly against the worktop, one leg crossing the other. She flicked her pony tail over her shoulder before examining her nails.

She'd broken in, probably disguised as the old man Danni had spied.

'If thatsh your idea of poetry, I wouldn't give up your day job.'

An expression of mock surprise. She stood up straighter, resting her palms on the solid wood bench-top behind her.

'Oh. Fancy that. Your speech is getting better. Pity you'll never live long enough to have that pretty face all better. As for Marky-Warky, he won't be too bothered; problems of his own, I believe.'

I stepped up to the doorway.

'Where is he, you bitch? And my parentsh?'

She waved her arms. 'Mumsy and Daddykins. Upstairs having a sleep.' She nodded towards two syringes on the worktop. 'I don't bear them any ill-will. You and Marky-Warky, though? That's different. Mark is . . . I don't remember exactly where. Some grass, a tree or two? I dumped him from that junk-heap car of his in the middle of nowhere. Some hills, a mountain? Who cares? Some isolated place where no one will find him before he freezes to death, that's a fact.'

Despite her past lies, I believed her. Slowly I reached for the police radio on the hall table.

'Naughty, naughty. Throw it over here, Kim . . . ber . . . ly.' Her tone was still sing-songy. Was she on some drug?

'What?'

'That radio. I see it in the mirror behind you.'

Damn. I'd forgotten about that mirror.

'Do not try to turn it on.'

Carefully I picked it up, slewing it across the tiled floor. 'What now, Rhonda? Going to blonde me to death?'

Without warning, Rhonda became a raging madwoman, producing a metal bar from behind her. A wheel nut wrench, presumably from Mark's car. Gnashing her teeth, she pounded the bar onto the radio again and again, shattering it and the tiles around it. Ceramic chips flew everywhere including her face, causing a trickle of blood to darken her cheek.

I gulped. First rule of policing; do not antagonise the bad guy. I'd never make that mistake again. If I survived this time.

Rhonda calmed immediately, panting but resuming her menacing charm. I'd seen capricious people in the past, vacillating between nicer-than-pie and manic, but this woman took the biscuit.

She was foaming at the mouth, her eyes those of a woman possessed. Sensuously, she put a fingertip to the blood on her face, inspected it then touched it to the tip of her tongue.

Rhonda was seriously barking mad. The trouble was, she still had that lug-wrench clasped in her hand. I had to keep her talking. Those two officers outside would surely realise things were amiss when I didn't return with their drinks. The Sergeant was armed. I'd seen a gun in his shoulder holster.

'Why me and Mark? Why kill ush?'

She shrugged. 'You upset my plans. Look at you. Compared to me, you're a nothing. I'm more intelligent, stronger and so, so much more beaut ... i ... ful. All I wanted was my baby girl back. That Candice didn't deserve her *and* all that money. I saw a photo of her family in the society pages. I could see she had my daughter so I took her back. And now you and that frozen boyfriend of yours have stolen her again. I hate you, Kim . . . ber . . . ly. And now you're going to die.'

She raised the weapon to lunge at me. I sidestepped her easily, whacking her with my elbow. She spun around, faster than I expected. I was backed into a corner.

Rhonda bared her teeth before hurling herself at me once more, the bar aimed at my head. I raised my left arm though I knew it was futile. I heard her maniacal shout, felt the whoosh of air on my face as I braced myself, eye closed.

Bang! The metal bar struck. I staggered back from the blow. Metal to metal. From under my jumper, two halves of my bracelet clattered to the floor. We stared at the remnants.

'What the . . . ?' Rhonda exclaimed. Although my wrist hurt like hell, the bracelet had protected it enough.

Recovering first, I swept one leg against her, knocking her off balance. Before she could right herself, I struck her chest with my right arm. She toppled backwards, the lug-wrench rolling from her hand.

I straddled her body, crushing her arms against her sides as she gasped in pain.

'You killed my Mark! You . . . killed . . . my . . . Mark . . . ' I struck her face with my good fist. Once, twice. All I could think of was Mark, dying out there alone. She'd pay for that, for the Bowens, parents and daughters, for Mum and Dad and for all she'd done to me. There was blood on my hand from her mouth. I didn't care.

There were sounds from the hall. I ignored them, lifting my fist a third time as tears ran down my face.

'That's enough, Kimberly. Stand down.'

Firm arms closed around me, easing me gently to my feet. Rhonda lay on her back, groaning. Did I do that to her? A part of me told me I had and that she deserved every blow. Another part felt ashamed. I watched Bill check Rhonda.

'She's breathing OK. Won't win any beauty contests for a while. Better shape than you, my girl,' he said to me as he put handcuffs on the Lollipop Lady before she revived too much. 'Good thing you pressed the panic button on the radio or we'd never have known you were in trouble.'

'I didn't. Rhonda must have set it off when she deshtroyed it,' I explained.

I could hear sirens. Bromyard police and ambulance.

Danni sat me on a dining chair and went upstairs. A door was unlocked, then she came back.

'Kimberly. Your parents are all right. Groggy, but all right.'

'What about Mark? She shaid he'sh lost some . . . '

'Mark is fine too. We found him.'

'But how? He wash stranded in the countryshide.'

Danni grinned. 'Suffice to say that is one super-smart boyfriend you have.'

16

It wasn't yet 1996. Well, not for another week. Still, I had my new diary and was already writing my resolutions for the New Year.

Top of the list was avoiding encounters with homicidal maniacs. Number two was to be more loving to my new boyfriend.

'I like that second one,' Mum said when I showed her.

'So, do I,' Mark commented then kissed me again. It was the end of Christmas Day and wrapping paper littered the lounge carpet. Lots of presents had been exchanged and a great deal of food eaten. Mark's family had returned home with a very tired but overjoyed Kylie, leaving the four of us sitting comfortably around. In the background the telly was on low, reminding me yet again that *Chitty*

Chitty Bang Bang had the most annoying sound track ever.

'Another mince pie, anyone?' Dad asked.

'Oh, go on. You've talked me into it,' Mark replied, sitting up. I snuggled up to him. His diet would start tomorrow, I decided. Let him have his ten thousand calorie treat if it kept him happy.

'You read well this morning, Kimberly,' Dad commented.

Yes, I had. My Bell's Palsy was dissipating much quicker than I dared hope. I could close both eyes, even smile and frown. I'd read the scripture at church, managing it in a comprehensible fashion.

The sling for my left arm had been decorated with tinsel. Mum and dad had no long-term health issues from the injections Rhonda had given them, and my bruises were fading.

As for Mark, he had survived his encounter with Rhonda relatively unscathed. She'd underestimated him when she'd pushed him out of the car to freeze to death, miles from anywhere. He'd had no coat, scarf or gloves but, on the coldest night of the year, my darling Mark had survived.

As Dad passed him a dish with mince pie and cream, Mark sat back and pressed a switch inside his shirt pocket. Rudolph's nose began glowing, illuminating the entire room in eerie redness.

'Good thing Rhonda didn't make you take off your jumper — otherwishe I'd probably need to be hunting for a new shweetheart right now.'

He gave me a cheeky grin. The new thin-rimmed glasses I'd bought him for Christmas were much more becoming. Amazing how quickly the spectacle maker had worked when he'd realised who I was.

'I'm not as dumb as I look, lover. Told you old Rudy here would make people notice me, and tonight is his last night being worn . . . at least until next Christmas.'

I said nothing. When next Christmas

came, his tastes would be more refined if I had anything to do with it. Instead I chose to find out the truth about that miraculous rescue of his.

'You never did tell me how you did it, Mark. Supposshe you show us all now.'

Dad turned off all the light including the Christmas tree. We were in total darkness.

Mark began. 'I was groggy from that sedative she gave me but aware enough to have an idea where she was driving. When she pushed me out of my car, I watched where she drove away until I saw the lights disappear. Then I turned ol' Rudy on.' He switched on the nose light on his chest.

'But it was jusht a red light. Why did all thosh farmersh and people go to inveshtigate?'

He reached into his shirt pocket and the light began flashing in a funny pattern. *Dot, dot, dot. Dash, dash, dash. Dot, dot, dot.*

'Morse Code. *SOS*.'

No wonder he'd attracted attention.

On that cold, moonless evening Rudy's powerful flashing nose must have been visible for miles down the hillside. He'd been rescued within twenty minutes.

Dad switched the lights back on again.

'Goodness. Didn't realise it was so late,' Mum declared, glancing at her watch. 'You two had best be going. That special present will be delivered to your flat in half an hour, Mark.'

'What special present?' Mark asked, puzzled.

'Yes, Linda. What special present?' Dad said before groaning in pain as he held his shin. Mum gave me a wink.

Mark's flat wasn't far away. He kept asking me about his belated gift yet I simply told him that he should be patient.

Once inside, I excused myself to go to the bathroom, returning minutes later in a skimpy negligée. Although difficult to arrange, the bright red ribbon and bow tied around me completed the ensemble.

'Well,' I said, posing in the doorway. 'Aren't you going to unwrap your gift?'

'You?? But I'm not ready. I . . . haven't exactly done this sort of thing before.' He blushed, his eyes semi-averted.

'Haven't done . . . ? Dear Lord. You're a — '

'Do not say the 'v' word, Kimberly.'

'I won't. However this will be your best present ever, Mr Rathaway.'

I switched off the main lights and headed for the bedroom, leading Mark by the hand. The bedside lamps were on and snow fell outside.

'And don't worry. I'll be gentle.'

★ ★ ★

By Easter, I was fully recovered from the debilitating episode in my life. Mark and I were searching for a home in Hereford to call our own.

Christmas and that dramatic search for Scarlett and Crystal almost seemed like a dream. But the two of us plus

Kylie often visited the Bowens. We'd become friends and I'm happy with that.

Due to my efforts tracing the girls, I was selected to be fast-tracked up the promotion ladder. Once that would have been all I wanted though, these days, there were more and more thoughts of me taking a career break in a few years to have children. That Mark will be a great father goes without saying. Me, as a mother? That's something I'm not so positive about, although I do relish the thought of finding out.

My colleagues at work and family insisted the palsy changed me for the better. Hopefully I was now more mature and tolerant of others.

I kept in touch with Ludavine and Mrs Wu. In fact, Mark and I are going to the Fish and Chippy tonight after work to sit and chat with her.

One final confession. When I mentioned I was totally recovered that isn't strictly true. There's a part of me I cherish that keeps me focused on those good things in life and that the future might not always be perfect.

Every morning, I glance in the mirror at Kimberly Frost (soon to be Kimberly Rathaway) . . . at her dark brown hair, dimpled cheeks and steel blue eyes. And then I remind myself of who I really am, with an ever-so-slightly crooked little smile.

We do hope that you have enjoyed reading this large print book.

Did you know that all of our titles are available for purchase?

We publish a wide range of high quality large print books including:
Romances, Mysteries, Classics
General Fiction
Non Fiction and Westerns

Special interest titles available in large print are:
The Little Oxford Dictionary
Music Book, Song Book
Hymn Book, Service Book

Also available from us courtesy of Oxford University Press:
Young Readers' Dictionary
(large print edition)
Young Readers' Thesaurus
(large print edition)

For further information or a free brochure, please contact us at:
Ulverscroft Large Print Books Ltd.,
The Green, Bradgate Road, Anstey,
Leicester, LE7 7FU, England.
Tel: (00 44) **0116 236 4325**
Fax: (00 44) **0116 234 0205**